THE GROVE

Robert John Percy

LUMINARE PRESS

WWW.LUMINAREPRESS.COM

Luminare Press
467 W 17th Ave
Eugene, OR 97401
www.luminarepress.com

LCCN: 2016939765
ISBN:978-1-937303-94-5

*This book is dedicated to all those who
appreciate a little mischief*

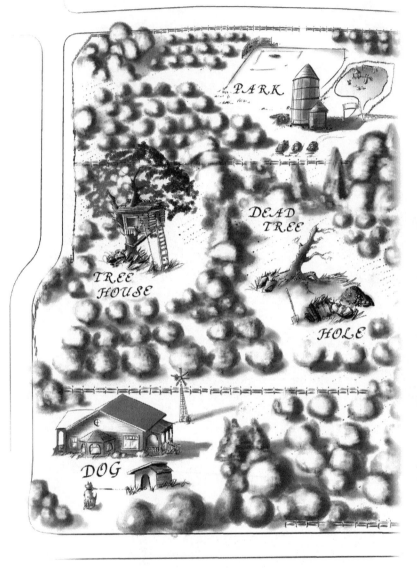

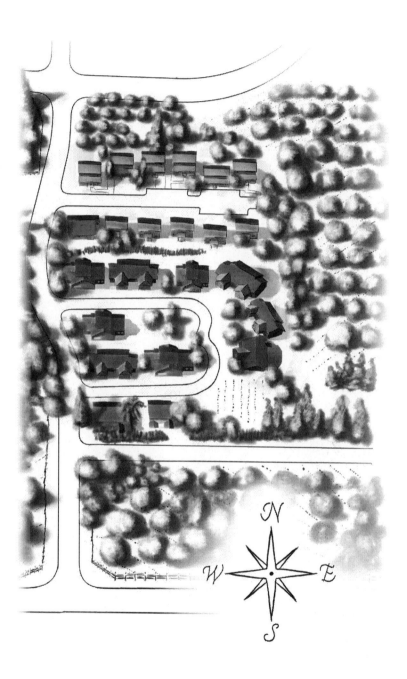

CHAPTER 1

Chipper Murphy figured it was in here somewhere. The corners of the two-car garage were dark with all manner of jumbled items blocking the way. With some effort he pushed past an old desk and spotted what he was looking for. Near the back of the garage, the family tent was where he stashed it last summer, buried under other camping equipment and a clump of old curtains. He leaned over as far as possible on top of a box of painting supplies, and placed his fingers around some of the heavy fabric and pulled it toward him. The thing must weigh forty pounds. It slept four people, maybe more. With a change of positions, Chipper gained the leverage he needed to lift the tent up on a nearby workbench. A final heave and it broke loose of whatever was holding it back, and then a thump as it landed atop the bench.

A deep breath and then he heaved it on a shoulder and carried it into the backyard. He dumped the tent in the middle of the lawn and walked back to the garage to look for tent poles.

He hoped this wasn't a waste of time.

As Chipper pounded the four stakes into the hard earth, he wondered if his friends Doog and Craig had talked to their parents yet. Doog's wouldn't care; they never did. But what about Craig's mother? She was strict. She might not consent. Craig had two older brothers, Jack and Thomas. They'd gotten caught by their mom smoking in their bedrooms. She went after them with a belt.

Today they were all lying to their parents. Part of their story was true; they'd begin the night in the tent. There was some guilt about not telling his parents.

Up went the center of the tent held by a shiny aluminum pole. He sensed his own uncertainty. Is this a good idea or not?

The side gate creaked and flew open. Doog Barnett raced into the backyard. "Need help?"

"Sure, hold this pole while I retighten the pegs."

Doog stepped inside the opening of the tent and took hold of the main support pole. "I've got it."

Doog was taller than the pole, so he ducked and let the middle of the tent rest on the post.

Chipper took one corner of the tent and a peg, and hammered away and asked Doog, "Can you do it? Can you come over?"

"Yeah, sure. I'm good. I just have to make sure I'm back home for church in the morning."

Doog's family was Catholic. They were especially proud these days because the nation had just elected a Catholic president of the United States. John Kennedy became president in 1961. Doog attended public school, same as Chipper. He was a year older, but they had both just finished sixth grade.

"What time does that start?"

Doog turned toward Chipper on the side of the tent. "Nine-thirty. Should be easy, right?"

"I think so. As long as we get back fast. Do you have an alarm clock to bring?"

"Maybe. I'll look around. What do we do if your parents find out we're not in the tent?"

"I don't know. Make something up, I guess."

One pound of the hammer and Chipper finished the peg attached to the last corner. The tent became rigid and stable and he called to Doog, "Come on out. It's good."

"It's cool inside. Lots of room. You heard yet if Craig's coming too? We have to all go. I hope he asks his dad, not his mom."

"What do we do if he can't?" Chipper asked as Doog appeared from around the corner of the tent.

"Wait till he can, I guess. Craig has to go, too."

Chipper wasn't surprised to hear this. Doog and Craig were best friends. They did everything as a pair. Chipper struggled when his family first relocated to the new neighborhood. He was left out of their activities for over a year. Even now, Chipper didn't always fit in.

"I'm going to his house and find out. Wanna come?" asked Doog.

Chipper hesitated. "No, go ahead. I'm setting up things for tonight. But let me know if he can't."

"Yeah, I will. I'll call ya if he can't go. I probably won't if Craig isn't coming."

Chipper looked at Doog, "Wait, we could still go, you know? Even if Craig can't."

Doog turned and said in a muted voice, "Let's wait till he can."

Chipper nodded. "Yeah. Whatever."

Doog left the backyard, the gate slamming after him.

Examining the tent again, Chipper worked himself inside and then lay on the canvas flooring. The temperature was already heating up inside with fresh air coming only through the zippered flap. Chipper closed his eyes and took a deep breath. He reflected on his plans for tonight. Was there something he'd overlooked? He'd picked Saturday night. Dad was around the house most of the day and tomorrow. Saturday was the safest night for sure. Dad would keep an eye on Mom. Normally it was enough. He hoped it was. Never really sure, Chipper asked himself if he could stop it all if suddenly Mom wasn't well tonight. Yes, it could be done. Had to many times before.

Chapter 2

The yellow wall phone rang twice before Chipper's sister Sandy answered. "Chipper! It's Doog! Are you here?"

"Yeah, I'm coming." He raced in from the backyard and in through the back door.

His sister stood waiting for him. Chipper reached out for the phone. "Hello? "

Doog's voice on the other end said, "Craig can't go. His cousins are here."

"Crap! You're kidding! They're much younger. What difference does it make?"

"Yeah. I don't know why his parents care if he stays around. He wants to do it. He can't. So what now?"

"Come over tonight anyway? The tent's set up." Looking to see if anybody was listening, Chipper quietly added, "We could always go to the grove like we planned. Or maybe not."

There was no response from Doog. With hesitation, he finally replied, "Yeah, we might do that. I guess I'll come down anyway. We can decide later."

"Ok, I'll see you here after dark. Come around back. I'll be in the tent."

"Right," said Doog. "I'll be down around nine."

Relieved, Chipper hung up the receiver and made his way to his bedroom. He was surprised that Doog didn't cancel.

In his bedroom, he looked for his small red transistor radio. It was still under his pillow where he had it last night, before falling asleep. He wanted comic books too. Pulling out the bottom drawer of his desk, he snatched a handful and set them next to the radio. What else? On the top shelf of the closet, he pulled down Stratego, a board game he played with his dad. The sound of the front door opening and closing caused him to glance out his side window toward the driveway. His Dad got inside his car and the engine roared to life. The big yellow Ford station wagon backed out of the driveway. Chipper noted that his mother wasn't in the car. As Chipper stood thinking, his father turned the corner and was gone.

He knew what he needed to do. Chipper opened his bedroom door and proceeded down the hallway into the living room. The television blared with his sister's favorite cartoon show. "Sandy. Seen Mom?"

"Backyard, I think. Not really sure."

He strode across the room to the patio slider, and carefully pulled the curtains apart.

His mother stood watering in the yard. With a garden hose in hand, she moved in among her flowerbeds.

He stepped back from the curtains. Doog was coming over later. He'd be humiliated if Doog found out. With no hesitation, he moved back past his sister. He slipped to the back of the house where the dryer was running. A persistent thump, thump echoed in the cramped utility room.

Carefully closing the door, Chipper hoisted himself up on the washing machine to reach the two cabinet doors. He peered into shelves where laundry soap and other cleaning supplies were kept. Not here anymore. The top shelf was empty, too. Behind him was a larger pantry. Back down, he hurriedly opened the double doors and looked inside. Jars, cans, boxes of rice, and other food stores took up the three top shelves. An empty grocery bag lay on the bottom shelf. A receipt was still inside. Chipper read over the list of purchases. In the middle of the list was the word, liquor. Chipper put the receipt in the bag and placed it back on the lower shelf again.

Where is it? A last glance at the pantry, then he backed out through the door to the kitchen and strode to his room. Out the window, his mother continued watering her plants.

The sun had vanished behind a row of tall eucalyptus trees. The heavy canvas tent had trapped the day's heat. His sleeping bag was laid out so that one end was near the opening. Propped on his elbows with his head sticking out the entrance, he placed the comic books nearby.

Kicking open the side gate, Doog entered carrying his stuff in a huge white duffle bag. "Hey Chipper! I'm here."

"Doog! Good. What do you have in there?"

"All kinds of things. Let me get the sleeping bag out first and I'll show ya."

Doog held the bag upside down. Out dropped a camouflage patterned sleeping bag and with it, lots of smaller objects. Doog threw the bag into the back of the tent and sat next to Chipper. He began picking through his pile. "I brought this." He held up a bone-handled knife. "You never know."

"That's cool, Doog. It's a hunting knife?"

"Yeah, sorta. I've used it for fishing when we go camping. Got it for Christmas." Doog set down the knife and reached for a long metal flashlight. "This has a lot of power and I just changed out the batteries." He clicked it on and shone the light on the inside of the darkening tent. If we go tonight, it will be dark in that grove. I'm not even sure we could find the tree house without a flashlight."

"Okay. What else?"

Doog reached for a smaller sack. He felt around inside. "I brought cards, a watch, some M&M's, beef jerky, and Sweet Tarts. I also have the new issue of Mad. Plus, my toothbrush. My mom made me bring it. So stupid."

"I brought some food, too," said Chipper. Stretching back behind him, he held a brown bag. "I've got corn nuts, chips, two hard boiled eggs, and Oreos."

Doog shrugged. "Eggs? I guess. I like eggs."

"Yeah, my mom saw all the other cookies and stuff I had and told me to take them too. You know, healthy and all that."

Doog proceeded to drag his belongings inside the tent. He plopped his pillow at the end of his bag nearest the zippered opening and set his Mad magazine out in front of him.

"I love Mad. I read every issue. Have you seen the back page this month?"

"No. Show me."

Doog turned to the very last page and folded it in half. By doing so, a new cartoon character was created.

"Cool."

"I always read Spy vs. Spy first."

He reached over and opened the pack of jerky. "Here, you want some?"

"Yeah, thanks." Chipper bit hard into the spicy meat stick. "Mmm, that's good."

"It's teriyaki. My favorite."

Doog turned the flashlight back on and found a comfortable position on his stomach. He started turning the pages of Mad.

Chipper opened his Batman comic to where he'd left off.

The interior of the tent cooled with the evening air. Doog's flashlight aimed a beam of light at his magazine. Chipper placed his comic near Doog's light. Looking over at him, Chipper asked, "So, should we go or not?"

"I don't know. We planned this with Craig. It was sorta his idea."

"Yeah, I know. We could just go out and back again. Not spend the night."

Staring down, Doog said, "We could. I'd feel better if it was three of us. I was in the groves at night once and it was spooky, and I couldn't see at all. I didn't like it."

"Yeah, me too. I cut through the orchard after dark on my way home from baseball practice once. I thought it would be easy, but it wasn't. I was sorta lost."

"We do have a flashlight, though. It'll help."

"I'll go if you will."

Doog sat up. "Man, I wish Craig were here. Okay, okay we can do it. To the tree house and back. But what about your parents?"

His parents would be getting ready for bed. They might read for a while.

"We need to wait. What time is it?"

Doog pushed open the tent flap; the lights in the house were out. The neighborhood had gone quiet. A faraway automobile engine reverberated as it accelerated away.

"I've got a clock in my bag. It runs on batteries. Just a sec."

Rummaging in his stuff, Doog pulled out the clock. "It's 10:05."

"We should wait till all the lights are out."

A noise close by caught their attention. A long squeak came from the side of the house.

"Did you hear that?" Doog whispered. A soft brushing sound and then footsteps. Doog reached for his flashlight.

"Doog! Chipper! It's me, Craig."

CHAPTER 3

Craig!" Doog blurted. "How'd you get out? Can you stay?"

Craig climbed through the tent opening and fell on his knees, panting and out of breath.

"I wanted to go so I jumped out my bedroom window. I pretended to go to sleep, but waited till it was quiet and then ran all the way here."

"You're kidding! What if your parents find out?" asked Chipper.

"They won't. They never check on me anymore. I want to go to the tree house like we said we would. Were you still going?"

"We were just planning," said Doog, "but we weren't going for the whole night, just out and back. Should we stay till morning now?"

Looking around, Chipper added, "You don't have a sleeping bag."

"No way I could get it. It's warm out. Can I use someone's pillow at least?"

"Here's mine." Chipper handed his pillow to Craig.

"Then I'm good. Let's go!"

Doog and Chipper reacted in a chorus. "Yes!"

They waited for the house lights to go dark and then rolled up the sleeping bags. They threw the food and candy into a paper sack and Chipper placed it inside his sleeping bag. Doog held the flashlight. Craig crawled from the tent grasping Chipper's pillow. Next, Doog dragged his big bag with Chipper following him.

Pass the patio, all dark and silent, then the gate, opening and closing. It banged shut, freezing them for a moment. Someone giggled, Chipper, trying not to laugh out loud, shushed Doog who started to laugh again, but held back.

On the sidewalk in front of the house, Chipper asked Doog, "You have the flashlight?"

"Yeah. Should I turn it on?"

"Not now," said Craig. "Wait till we're in the grove."

Up and down the street, porch lights were turned off for the night. Ahead, the blackness of the vast orange grove was a half block away and they sped up passing the last streetlight on the block. The three figures huddled together, shuffling down the street with their bags and pillows tucked under their arms.

Moving across the street, a line of eucalyptus trees separated them from the orchard. Chipper looked back toward his neighborhood once more. Across the street from Chipper's house was another streetlight. Was someone standing there on the edges of the light beam?

"Doog, Craig—stop a sec," Chipper whispered. "Look over by the light."

From between the tall thin eucalyptus, Doog and Craig turned and peered back.

"Yeah, let's go before they see us," said Craig.

Ducking, Chipper worked his way past the branches and piles of thin bark that littered the ground. He glanced behind looking for the figure by the light. The sidewalk was empty now.

The expansive grove stretched out ahead.

"Time for the flashlight?" Doog asked.

Craig whispered back. "Wait till we're in a few rows just in case somebody's still close by.

"Good idea 'cause I saw a person over there. I'm positive," added Chipper.

"Me too," said Craig. "They can't see us now."

Cautiously, they moved through the freshly plowed rows of orange trees. The dark green branches were full of fruit and the scent of ripening oranges freshened the air. Doog clicked on the flashlight. A beam of light bounced off the ground, then the trees.

Another long line of eucalyptus trees loomed ahead, separating one section of grove from another. The towering trees with the strong pungent smell were planted in straight rows completely surrounding the smaller orange trees.

Lines of eucalyptus marked the boundary of one irrigation system from another, and when the wind blew, the larger trees protected the smaller fruit trees. When the wind was especially powerful, dry desert gusts blew the big trees over. A fallen eucalyptus was perfect for energetic fort-building by local kids. Then one day, workers for the Grove Man would come to cut it up. Forts disappeared into a dump truck.

Chipper's stomach felt queasy. Too much candy. Nerves. They were close to the tree house. Far from the backyard tent now. The only noise was their feet trudging through the soft dirt. He was doing something others his age had never done. It reminded him of Roger Bell. Roger's family lived among a small grove with a huge tree house on the acreage behind the farmhouse. Chipper knew Roger often spent nights during the summer sleeping in it. He admired Roger Bell more than just about anybody and hoped for a chance to tell him about this night's adventure.

"Is this where we turn?" Doog pointed the flashlight at a stand of tightly bunched trees on the left.

The group changed direction. Passing between trees meant pushing the branches aside and avoiding the thorns.

"Can anyone see the tree?" Chipper peered ahead.

"It's right there, see it?" replied Craig.

"I don't think so." Doog pointed the beam of light farther ahead. "Everything looks so different. We have to get to the end of this line of eucalyptus."

Craig stopped and looked around. "Okay. You're right."

Chipper was thirsty. They hadn't brought a canteen of water. He could grab an orange that hung close to the ground. These oranges had thin skins and were used to make juice. They made your hands sticky when you tried to peel them.

Suddenly, Doog stopped. "Did someone bring a key?

"Oh crap, I forgot mine!" said Chipper.

Craig halted and looked at both Chipper and Doog. "How were you guys getting in?"

Embarrassed, Chipper said, "I didn't even think about it. Jeez so stupid."

Craig reached into his pocket. "Good thing I brought mine." He held up his gold key.

Feeling relieved, Chipper hurried down the line of trees looking for the outline of the thick avocado branches that held the tree fort they had finished building days before.

"There it is. Up ahead." Chipper hurried his pace.

Doog and Craig sped up to a trot.

Nothing seemed the same as in the daytime. Staring at the dark structure in the tree above, he saw that the tree house received no light at all from the moonlight. The branches and leaves blanketed the whole thing in an umbrella of deep shadow. Dropping the bags at the base of a tree, Craig went up first to open the lock.

"Doog. Hand me the flashlight."

Standing on the top stair he pointed it at the hatch door.

"Hey!" he shouted down. "The door is open!"

"It couldn't be!" shouted Doog back. "I'm sure I locked it yesterday. I'm pretty sure, anyway."

Craig called from inside. "It's okay. Hand up the bags."

Craig shone the flashlight around the four walls. A few candy wrappers remained on the floor from days before, and there were loose nails and a hammer they'd left. Doog climbed up the ladder rungs to the large limb underneath the floor. Chipper stayed on the ground and passed the two sleeping bags to Doog. Being the last one up, he used the steps nailed to the tree, hefted himself through the hatch, and into the confines of their fort. The branch that held them swayed when they moved about. Craig stood near one of the four open window spaces and, projected the light all around the orchard that encircled the broad branches of the enormous tree. The light bounced off the ground in the distance and lit for an instant all the trees it touched.

Chipper looked out a window as Craig directed the beam down the rows of trees as far as he could.

"That light is pretty easy to see from far off. Maybe you should turn it off?"

"Yeah, you're right." Craig clicked off the flashlight. "You never know who might be out here. I always hear weird stuff from my brothers. They'd think we were crazy to be out here."

"Man, it's dark," said Chipper. "Can't see anything."

"Yeah! I can't believe we're doing this," said Doog, a little too loud. "Have you guys ever done anything totally alone? No adults around?"

Chipper didn't answer. This was new. Maybe a bad idea. What about his parents? What would they do if they found out he was gone from the backyard? Call the police?

Craig broke in, "I have. My brother took me up to Big Bear Lake with a bunch of his friends. I had so much fun. Some girls came over from another campground and hung out with us."

What were past examples of independence? He had no older brother or even an older sister. He had a younger sister he paid little attention to.

Doog remembered something. "I have a cousin in San Diego, and one time he and I were in a sailboat race. He knows how to sail, and I helped, too. We got to sleep on the boat while it was moored out in the bay. I sailed by myself a couple of times. When I get some money, I'm buying a sailboat."

"All seems okay in here." Craig turned back to his friends. "I'd sure like to know why the trap door was open, though. Come on, Doog, you must have forgotten to lock it."

"I did not!" shot back Doog. "I always lock it when I

leave. It's always been locked before, hasn't it?"

"Well, I guess so," conceded Craig.

Doog was responsible for being the last out and locking the door.

Craig found his sleeping bag and spread it on the floor. Doog put his next to him and then emptied his big bag. It deposited his sleeping bag, comic books, chocolate bar, toothbrush, and his knife onto the wood floor.

Chipper remembered the sack. Inside were a hardboiled egg, a piece of jerky, and Doog's watch. He set the food near where is head would lay. Too warm to be inside the bag, he lay on top. Doog did the same.

"Geez, I never noticed this floor was so hard." Craig looked at Chipper. "I didn't think it would be this bad. At least I have a soft pillow and it's warm."

"I'll trade spots," Chipper said. "I've got a bent nail under me."

Craig laughed. "You're the one who probably bent it."

Chipper laughed, too.

He moved his body in different positions trying to find some comfort.

Across from him Doog lay quietly in the darkness, and asked, "Anyone know any spooky stories?"

Chipper's heart sank a little. Scary stories were the last thing he wanted to hear right now.

"Have you guys heard the stories about some old guy called Dirty Charlie?" asked Craig.

"Who?" responded Doog and Chipper at the same time.

"Dirty Charlie, the crazy man, who had a home in the groves before he killed somebody and was sent to a prison hospital, or something like that. He owned lots of property and never took a bath. He is rich, though," said Craig.

"How can that be?" Chipper hoped the story wasn't true.

"It's true," returned Craig. "My brother Tom told me all about him. He's out of jail now and sometimes grove workers see him wandering around. My brother says he carries a big knife, and he's dangerous."

For a while, no one spoke. Then, Chipper said, "Well, I hope your brother was just making that up."

Doog nodded in agreement, but then announced, "Tomorrow we should start searching for him. Let's see if we can find out where he lives and stuff."

"Yeah, good idea, Doog. I'll ask my brother if he knows any more about him," responded Craig.

"Well maybe," said Chipper halfheartedly. "Why do we want to find a crazy man with a knife?"

Doog snorted and laughed.

"'Cause. Why not?" said Craig.

Doog shifted around. "Who's waking up early so we can be back at the tent before Chipper's dad gets up?"

"I will wake up as soon as it starts getting light out," said Craig.

"Are you sure?" asked Chipper. He'd never woke that early in the summer time.

"Yeah, I'll wake you," responded Craig. "Where is your clock, Doog? Hand it to me."

Doog passed the clock to Craig who set it between he and Chipper.

"I'll try to wake up in time, too." Chipper squirmed lower into his bag trying to get comfortable. Starting out on his stomach like at home, put his face against the hard floor and then flipped onto his back.

His two friends lay in lumps on either side of him. Thirteen-year-old Doog was the oldest by almost a year. He'd taken the second grade again. Doog still didn't do very well in school. His grades were a little lower than Chipper, who was a better-than-average student. Doog was a far better athlete than Chipper, though, and actually that seemed more important. His real name was Douglas, but everyone called him Doog, which was started by an older sibling when he was four years old.

Craig, taller than Chipper, was smart and athletic, too. He was popular in class, and girls liked him. They gossiped about him and chased him around the schoolyard. In sixth grade, he had a real girlfriend. Craig knew about important things, which he learned from his older brothers. Doog and Craig had been friends for a long time before Chipper moved to the neighborhood three years ago. When he first saw them, he thought they were brothers. They both had light brown hair and eyes. In the summertime, they often dressed alike and wore tennis shoes without socks.

Doog and Craig were his best friends. There was the one quarrel. The problem started with Craig, but then a falling out with Doog quickly followed. They were loyal to each other more than they were to Chipper. The incident had passed quickly, but he was careful to avoid conflict with them again.

Chipper envied that both Craig and Doog had older brothers. They seemed to know more about a lot of stuff. Brothers could make the world seem safer somehow, although both Craig and Doog complained they also picked on them. Made life hard sometimes. Neither Craig nor Doog had the problems he did with school toughs like eighth grader Rodney Kruger. If he had an older brother, he would ask him to scare Rodney. No, Rodney Kruger would never call Chipper "Chipmunk" again.

The comfortable slumber of half-sleep enveloped him as he envisioned an older brother coming to his support the next time Kruger pushed him around.

Chapter 4

First came the soft light of the sun's rays appearing on the tallest nearby trees. The cool grayness around the tree house took on a silver glow. The night's cooler temperature wouldn't last long in mid-June. Crows were calling loudly to each other, and it was that and the hard surface below him that woke Chipper. The briefest thought asked, where am I? Then, memories tumbled out one after another. The tent, Craig, and Doog. Walking in the dark. What time was it? He felt like he could fall back to sleep. Craig said he would wake up. Where was Doog's watch? Next to him, Craig lay curled up. Nothing but a pillow. Doog on the other side. The watch lay near, and Chipper saw the time. Six a.m. He yawned, sleep tempting again.

He rolled away, and laid on his other side. On the floor next to his face was a large knothole. Chipper could see through it to the ground. Scattered leaves, a branch, an avocado fallen from the tree. Something white on the ground next to the avocado. An egg. The hard-boiled egg he'd brought. It must have fallen through the hole. The egg showed no cracks from its fall. Was it still edible?

He closed his eyes welcoming sleep again. A sound. Opening one eye, he peered through the knothole. Both the egg and avocado disappeared from view. Confusion, then fear. Instinctively, he stopped breathing. A figure blotted Chipper's view of the ground. Somebody was bending over to pick up the egg. Watching closely now as the intruder moved and looked left then right. From his vantage point directly above, he saw a cap, rough coat, large shoulders, and leather shoes. Chipper remained motionless as the person turned to face the tree trunk and the steps to the tree house. The intruder's eyes panned the trunk in and followed the steps to the first limb and then he tilted his head eyeing the tree house. Chipper moved his head away from the hole just before the figure looked. Too late to see the face. The sound of a slow shuffling began as whomever it was moved around. He could look through the hole again, but hesitated.

If only Craig and Doog were awake. The sound of their gentle breathing continued as they slept. Need to listen closely. Be very still. He counted to ten and leaned cautiously back to look through the hole and saw nothing. Both the avocado and the egg were gone. With one eye, he tried to expand the sightlines visible through the knothole. Nothing. Gone?

Slow to take a breath, he needed air. He leaned to wake Craig, but froze. Was there movement under him? The trap door. He was lying on it.

He felt it now, pushing upward. He pressed hard on the plywood door. He glanced at Doog's knife. If only his friends were awake. Did the person know he was here? Keep pushing until he gives up. Would he give up? The sounds of wood cracking and a heavy thud as though someone had jumped to the ground. Was he leaving? No movement. Listening intently, he started breathing again.

This time he would wait. How would he know for sure? Were those footsteps? Leaves crunching? It seemed to be farther away and then the crows again.

Craig stirred. Chipper sat up, alert. In a soft, but urgent voice he said, "Craig, wake up."

Craig opened his eyes and looked at Chipper. "What's the matter?" he asked.

Chipper put his finger to his lips and said even softer, "Shhhh, quiet."

Craig propped on an elbow and looked at Chipper, puzzled.

"Someone just tried to get in. I was sitting on top of the door so they couldn't."

Doog heard Chipper this time and lifted his head. "What?" he drawled sleepily.

"I'm not sure. I think he's gone."

Craig looked up toward the large open windows, saying nothing, but listening for unusual sounds. He looked back at Chipper with a questioning face.

"What are you talking about?" asked Doog.

Craig rose from the floor. Pointing at the windows, he said, "Take a peek above your head and I'll check from over here."

Chipper worked his way to the wall and peered around the corner of the opening. An inch at a time, he moved his head further into the big square that looked over the grove. Just trees in every direction.

Doog pulled himself out of his sack and made his way

to the window next to Craig. "What am I looking for?"

"Anybody. Someone walking away. I'm not sure," whispered Chipper.

"Nothing over here," said Craig. "Are you sure, Chipper? Are you making this up?"

Doog chimed in, "I don't see anything. What happened?"

Craig turned toward Chipper. "Are you putting us on? Because man, you better not be."

Chipper looked at Craig with a deep frown and wide eyes, shook his head and Craig stopped talking.

"Somebody tried to get in. No lie."

Chippers' hands were trembling. He felt warmer than he should be. Sweat sat on his brow. "Let's go. Get out of here."

"Yeah, what time is it?" asked Doog.

"It's early, but we need to go," Chipper answered.

"Okay, this is too weird. I'm ready right now. Get your things." Craig picked up the pillow and scanned out the window again.

Doog started packing his big bag. "They were coming up through the door? Who was it? Did you see anything?"

"Later," said Chipper. "When we get home."

Chipper slowly lifted the door and looked below for movement. Just the ground. Doog went through the opening first, then Chipper. Craig tossed the bags to him and in a moment all three boys were out of the tree.

"See that egg?" Chipper pointed to the place where it lay on the other side of the tree trunk. He picked it up and must have dropped it again. "I saw the egg before I saw him."

"I believe you. Let's go," said Doog.

Running more than they walked, they only slowed once. The usual line of eucalyptus trees marked the end of the grove and the beginning of Chipper's street. Early Sunday morning. Peaceful, quiet, and still. Most were sleeping. Emerging from the trees they ran the rest of the way to Chipper's house. Passing through the gate, would a furious dad be waiting by the tent.

The tent and everything in the backyard seemed unchanged.

Once inside, Chipper and Doog rolled out their bags again.

Doog spoke first. "Are you sure it wasn't the Grove Man out there? You know that he works early in the morning. Or it could have been one of the workers."

The Grove Man was a term everyone used to describe just about any of the many employees of the grove owner. They often drove around in white trucks and always seemed to be carrying a shovel. Grove Men rarely said anything to kids playing among the trees. Don't pick the oranges, though.

Chipper stretched out on his bag, "No," he said thoughtfully, "There was something that makes me think it was someone else. I forgot about it until now, but the guy had on like, nice leather shoes. My dad calls them wingtips. He wears them to work and church."

"You mean he was dressed up?" Craig asked.

"No, only the shoes. He had on a big black coat, or it seemed like it. I couldn't really see the rest of him. I didn't see his face."

"Maybe it was that Dirty Charlie guy or a grove bum," suggested Doog.

Craig shook his head. "Not with hard shoes like you go to church in. Grove bums never have nice shoes, but I don't know about Dirty Charlie. I'll have to ask my brother. I better go. Nobody's up early on Sunday, but we have company. Come see me later today."

With a wave of his hand Craig jumped up and exited the tent.

"I'm sure glad Craig came," said Doog.

"Yeah, me too."

"I'm tired," said Doog. "I'm going back to sleep."

"Okay, Doog. If I'm asleep when you leave, I'll see you later on."

"You weren't making up anything, right Chipper?"

"No, I wish I was."

There was a sound from the house. A door closed. Maybe his father was up and looking for the Sunday paper on the front porch.

Doog peered at Chipper. "Did you hear that?"

"Yeah. Probably my Dad."

Both now lay flat in their bags. Silent. Eyes closed, Chipper took a deep breath. It felt safe again. By the time Chipper's father came to check the tent, they were asleep.

CHAPTER 5

Before long, the heat inside the green canvas tent woke Chipper. They collected their things and crawled out to the cooler fresh air.

"I better get going." Doog hefted his bag onto his shoulder.

"Meet at Craig's later, right?"

"Yeah, after lunch? I wonder if he made it back to his bedroom without getting caught. I gotta mow the lawn and other stuff. My dad will have a list of chores today," said Chipper.

"Me too. It's Sunday. I probably need to clean my room. See ya later at Craig's."

"See ya, Doog." Chipper walked toward the back door. "Oh, and we're not telling anyone about last night, right?"

"No way. Not me."

"Okay, see you later."

Doog exited the yard and Chipper opened the back door to the house.

Wandering into the kitchen, all was quiet. Was anyone home? From the fridge he took a carton of milk and reached for his favorite cereal. The Sunday Times was scattered on the dining table. Where's the sports section? Opening to the baseball scores for yesterday's games, Chipper checked to see how the Dodgers and Twins did. The Dodgers were the local southern California team, but his favorite was Minnesota. He wasn't even sure why. He'd been a baseball fan for many years, but he like football better.

The cereal tasted good and he poured another bowl. He looked up from the newspaper and stopped reading. What about last night? There was the darkness of the grove, Craig's story about Dirty Charlie. Most of all he pondered the mystery of waking up to someone trying to get into the tree house. He'd been afraid. They hadn't gotten in, but what if they had?

Cereal finished, Chipper rinsed the bowl in the sink. The grass in the backyard was deep. Better get going. The tent would have to come down.

The mower started with a roar. Pushing through the thick blades was hard work. Plus, he'd need to rake all the cut grass because the mower was older and without a grass catcher. Once the mowing was done, he'd sweep the patio and sidewalks. All this would take at least an hour. When he was nearly through, his mother slid open the glass door to the patio. She sat in a lounge chair, sunglasses on, sipping a glass of orange juice, enjoying the sunny day. She waved to Chipper and he waved back.

Maybe it was a good time to ask about Dirty Charlie. He stopped raking and yelled to her across the yard, "Hey Mom, have you ever heard of someone called Dirty Charlie?

"Who?"

"Dirty Charlie," he repeated. "Craig was talking about

him. Heard a story from his brother. He's supposedly a rich old guy who dresses in crummy clothes and owns a bunch of orchards, or something like that. He's like an orchard bum."

Chipper's mother turned to look at him. "A rich bum? I'm not sure there is such a thing. Craig's brother is probably kidding him. Did he say anything else?"

"He might have gone to jail, too."

His mother smiled. "Sounds made up. Brothers sometimes do that."

"Hmm, maybe he is. I told him that." Chipper was confident his mother was right. He started raking again. Craig probably believed anything his brother says. Pretty stupid.

His mother had brought a book to read. Chipper thought about how much he enjoyed his mother when she was like this. Normal. She was smart, funny and seemed happy. Confusing. He didn't understand it.

Doog's house was four doors from Chipper's. Chipper usually went by there first before going to Craig's further down the street. Today, Chipper went directly to Craig's.

All the homes along this part of his neighborhood were familiar. He knew who lived in each one. The trees and shrubs planted amongst the newer homes were small and created a modest amount of shade. In front of the Cabrerra's house, he stopped. Their lawn needed mowing, and edging too. He looked up at the doorsteps. The Cabrerra's didn't have children living at home anymore and were often out of town. They paid Chipper generously a few times to work in their yard. Chipper thought about going to the door and asking about the lawn. While he stood debating this idea, someone called his name.

"Hey Chip, what's up?"

Chipper turned knowing there was only one person who called him Chip, and there was a familiar face, Kristy Mason. She was sunbathing on her roof. With a large beach towel laid out and the little yellow transistor radio Kristy always carried with her. A song was playing by a new singing group called The Beach Boys. They were very popular in southern California. She also had a paperback book and some tanning oil.

"Kristy, what are you doing?" yelled Chipper.

"What does it look like? I'm tanning. How do you think it looks?" Wearing a white bathing suit, Kristy stood and showed Chipper her tan. Kristy was nearly always tan; she was one of those people who tanned easily.

"Yeah, you are really dark, Kristy. Are you burned?"

"I use a lot of tanning oil," said Kristy, "and I don't stay here too long. It's easy getting up, but getting down is harder. Hey Chip, I'm mowing Cabrerra's later, so don't get any ideas. I already talked to Mrs. Cabrerra."

"Oh, okay, if you need help, let me know."

"Sure maybe, she answered turning onto her stomach. See you later, Chipper."

He waved and continued walking. After some paces he turned and looked back at Kristy on the roof. Not sure about her. She could be like a best friend, and next time, she'd ignore him. There was something about her though. He knew that, but she was entering eighth grade and Chipper would only be in seventh. At school she'd say hi. Always those older boys around. She lived close-by though.

He'd known her for two years. He enjoyed looking at her hair. It was long, and sort of a brownish red. Most of the time, she wore it braided, or in one long ponytail. Chipper never tired of looking at it. Kristy had P.E. class at the same time as him last school year. He saw her sometimes out on the playing fields. She was quite athletic. She took dance classes of some kind, had plenty of friends, too. In fact, she was one of the most popular girls in school. Kristy had caused a big uproar by going steady once in sixth grade with a boy two years older. This only lasted a week, but everyone knew, including her mother, who put an end to it with a call to the boy's parents. Kristy was still angry about that. Chipper never had a girlfriend. He liked Kristy and was happy she was his friend.

Craig's was the only two-story house on the block. A big oval swimming pool, built last summer, was centered in the back yard. The garage door was open and he made his way through to the rear door. Chipper found his friend cleaning leaves out of the pool. Eucalyptus leaves, long and narrow from a row of trees behind the yard.

Craig saw Chipper. "I'll be done in a sec. Have you seen Doog yet?"

"No, I came straight here," replied Chipper. "Did you get back in without being caught?"

"Barely. Right after I crawled in the window, one of my cousins came to see if I was up yet. What about you guys?"

"We fell asleep. What are we doing today?"

"Not sure. That was weird this morning. Who was that?"

"Who knows? Probably a grove bum wandering around. Saw the tree house."

"Hope so. You were pretty scared, huh?" Craig netted another cluster of leaves. "I thought we were going looking for Dirty Charlie. Right?"

Chipper hesitated. "I guess, but I asked my mother about him this morning. Mom thinks maybe your brother made it up to scare you and there's no such person."

Craig stopped working, looking at Chipper. "Hey, Chipper, I just talked to Thomas again. He says it's true, and I believe him. Your mother doesn't know everything, you know."

"Well, you can believe it if you want," returned Chipper, "but I don't know."

"Okay, maybe just Doog and I will go." Craig looked away. He dipped the long net into the water again, moving farther from Chipper.

Chipper couldn't think what to say. Why argue? Craig believed everything Thomas said. No changing that.

"I guess I could look, too. There are parts of the grove I've never explored. Then later we could go back to the tree house and check on it. Is this all you have to do?"

"I don't know," Craig mumbled back. No one spoke while he captured more floating leaves. "Actually, Doog wanted me to come over. If we go into the groves, we'll come get you."

Chipper nodded. He didn't like anyone challenging what the older brother said, should have known that. "Well, maybe I'll see you tomorrow." Chipper walked toward the side gate.

"Yeah, okay," he said, still looking down at the pool. "If we try to find Dirty Charlie, where should we look?"

"Don't know. Way out past our tree house somewhere. Or other groves."

"Yeah, maybe I'll see what Tom thinks."

"Okay, let me know what he says. Get me if you go." Chipper moved slowly toward the front yard. On the way through an open garage door, he passed a kneeling Thomas working on his motorcycle. Greasy tools lay on the cement floor. Thomas grunted something and Chipper nodded back.

Walking back the way he'd come, Chipper passed Kristy's house again and his eyes scanned the rooftop. A white towel but no Kristy. Disappointed.

Then the familiar voice, "Hey Chip, over here." Kristy was by the side of the house, climbing down onto the fence top.

She lowered herself on her stomach until her feet found the fence and then carefully eased off the roof until she was standing on the fence top. With a whoop, she jumped onto the ground from there.

"Too hot up there now," said Kristy, "I am going to wash off with the hose, I'll be right back."

Chipper crossed to Kristy's side of the street and slowed his walk.

She came back from around the corner. Chipper smiled as she asked, "Was Craig home?"

"Yep, but he's working in the yard and stuff."

Kristy sat on the street and looked up at him. "Hey Chip, I've been told you have a cool tree house out in the grove. Is it true?"

Chipper pretended surprise. "Who told you that?"

"Oh, come on, Chipper, everybody knows. They just aren't sure where it's at."

"I guess we do, but I can't tell you where it is. Craig, Doog, and I built it. Some people might try to wreck it."

Kristy made direct eye contact and said nothing. He sat next to her.

"C'mon Chip," she pleaded, "I promise not to tell, really I won't. I want to see it."

"You can't tell Doog and Craig I took you there."

"Yes. Of course."

"I promised to keep it a secret, but if you really want to go. I guess we could."

"Really? Let's go! Let me change, and I'll meet you at your house."

Chipper thought about that. It was mid-afternoon. Maybe it wasn't a good idea to have Kristy show up at the front door. "How about I'll meet you in ten minutes at the corner?" Chipper suggested.

"I'll be there!" She disappeared into her front porch.

Chipper stood and began walking home. His Dad's car was gone. Usually, Dad was home all day on Sunday, and that meant Mom would be okay. Maybe she had gone with him.

Inside, the sound of his sister's voice came from her room. Must be a friend with her. Entering the living room, he stopped and peered beyond the kitchen. On the far side, the door to the laundry room was shut. Movement, and cabinet doors opened and closed. Mom was behind the doors. He tensed and turned back toward his bedroom. He needed the key to the latch. Inside a drawer next to his bed he found it. Was Kristy already waiting?

Near the front door, his mother called, "Chipper, where are you off to?" Her voice was already changed.

"Nowhere." Ignoring the fear, he walked into the front yard to wait for Kristy. A quick glance back at the house. Was Mom behind him? Was she coming outside? He waited for her to appear. Nothing. Keep going.

Kristy appeared on the sidewalk. "I'm excited. Which grove is it in?"

"I think Ramos owns it. Just across Fruit Street."

"Where did you get the wood and stuff?"

"Doog's uncle works in construction. He saved us boards and gave us nails."

Looking to see if anyone was watching, they sprinted into the first row of trees.

He had awakened in the tree house that morning. Was the intruder gone, or still in the grove? Hadn't thought about that.

Soon, they were enveloped into the warm silence of hundreds of orange trees. The ground was dry and dusty, and between the rows of trees were irrigation ditches used to get water to each tree. Along each section was the long line of eucalyptus trees. Chipper recognized these big trees well and was looking for one that was shorter than the others. He would left turn and that would take him to the wooden fort.

He looked for a ripe orange to pick, and found one on a lower branch. Peeling the fruit, Chipper said, "There's more I haven't told you. We slept overnight out here."

"What!

"Yeah, really. Me, Doog, and Craig. Last night." Chipper told Kristy the whole story: the tent, Craig showing up, sneaking out of the yard, the intruder that morning.

"Can't believe you did that. Weren't you afraid?"

"Really scared. We ran the whole way back home."

"Nobody's done that before. Not the whole night."

Chipper looked down a long aisle of trees. "I guess he could still be here."

"Now you're scaring me."

"Sorry."

"Maybe we should be quieter."

"Yeah, I guess."

No talking now. Almost there. Scanning the trees up and down the straight aisles. Nothing unusual. It was always quiet and warm with only the sound of their feet shuffling through the chocolate brown dirt. The shorter eucalyptus ahead means turn left and follow a long line of taller trees. Some shade. The eucalyptus bark, like cinnamon shavings, littered the ground.

"Where is it?" Kristy searched the trees ahead.

Chipper stopped walking and pointed. "See the big tree?"

The avocado tree stood out. Far larger than any orange tree. More like a big oak.

"Wow, this is so cool." Kristy studied the floor of the tree house. "It's sorta like Roger Bell's."

"I've got to unlock the hatch."

Chipper climbed the steps on the tree trunk then fiddled with the latch and pushed it back so they could enter. Once she worked herself up and inside, Kristy peered out all four windows viewing the dark green orange trees below. "It must have been so spooky up here."

"It was. We had a flashlight. When it was off, it was totally black."

Again, he repeated the story of the morning's intrusion. Chipper showed Kristy how he'd pressed with his full weight on the trapdoor so the intruder couldn't get in.

"You want to climb on the roof? We can get up there."

"How?"

Chipper started out a window and then stepped on a big branch so he could heft himself up.

"You coming?" he called.

"Yes, of course." Kristy made her way to meet him.

"Cool here, isn't it?"

Christy laughed. "Yeah, but not as sturdy as the roof at home. Not that I don't trust your building skills. I like it better inside."

"Right. Me too. Especially if it's windy."

She reversed her steps back on the branch and in through the window. Chipper followed.

As Kristy eased herself inside, Chipper heard what sounded like an orange or dirt clod smack the solid plywood on the outer side of the tree house. Another bang and another loud splat. Oranges striking nearby. Puzzled, they ducked low on the floor and away from the windows. An overripe orange whizzed through a window and bounced off an inner wall, spraying rind in the air. Two more hits near the open windows sounded outside. Chipper tried to peek between the cracks in the wall. Somebody having fun. Hard to see much. Who was it?

Kristy looked at Chipper and mouthed, "What's going on?"

Chipper shook his head. "Can't see." A larger seam above him gave a better view. He saw them. "Crap. This is bad."

"Who?"

Lurking in the shadow of the tree was Benny Gross. Next to him was his friend, Rodney Kruger.

Chapter 6

"Hey Chipper, let us in. We know you're there. And Kristy, too."

Chipper recognized Kruger's voice.

"Yeah, we wanna see inside. What's the big deal?" added Benny, chuckling. Then he said, "I noticed you last night, with those two other kids."

Benny must have been the lone figure they'd seen before entering the grove. Bad luck.

"What should we do?" asked Kristy, worried.

Chipper closed the hatch and moved over to sit on it. "They can't get in."

Two more oranges bounced off the outside wall.

"C'mon Chipper, let us up." Rodney called. "We're going to keep throwing until you do."

Kristy yelled, "Go away."

"Let us in, Chipmunk, we just want to check out inside," added Benny.

"Forget it," Chipper yelled in return. "You guys will wreck it."

Kristy, red-faced, watched another dirt clod hit the

nearby wall. She stood and yelled, "Leave us alone. Get out of here!"

"Who are you, Kristy? Chipmunk's protector?" retorted Rod. "C'mon, Chipper, be a man."

Benny laughed.

Forlorn, Chipper frowned at Kristy who sat on the trap door. It couldn't be pushed open. What would happen if he allowed them in? What about Craig and Doog? Rod and Benny knew where the tree house was now, and they could come back at any time.

Chipper looked at Kristy. "Maybe we should just let them in and get out of here."

"It's okay with me. It's your place, but jeez, I hate those guys. They are such jerks."

Chipper stood and peeked out the window. Benny Gross was looking up. Chipper turned to Kristy. "Go ahead and open the door, and then let's leave fast."

Kristy bent to open the door when hard smack sounded behind her. Chipper howled, reacting to a golf ball size, unripe, orange hitting him under his right eye. The fruit rolled across the floor. Chipper bent with his hands on his face, cursing.

"Are you okay, Chipper?"

Groaning, he couldn't answer. A large red welt was forming under his eye.

Benny yelled again. "We're coming up, open the door."

"Forget it!" Kristy yelled. "You hit Chipper in the face, and he's hurt. Get out of here and leave us alone. We're not letting you in!"

Benny shouted, "I didn't hit him, Rod did, accidentally."

"Yeah, accidentally," chimed Rodney.

Hearing them snicker, Kristy reached for an orange they'd thrown and threw it back at them. "You're total jerks."

Chipper sat in the corner covering his cheek with one hand, trying to hold back tears. Angry, Kristy snatched the green orange from the floor, stood up and threw it back out the window toward Rodney Kruger.

"So you want a real fight, huh, Kristy? Okay, we'll see who wins. Let us know when you've had enough." Said Kruger.

"Yeah, you asked for it. Rod and I won't run out of oranges to throw."

Chipper said nothing. Kristy sank down in the corner. "Sorry, Chipper. Let me look at your face."

Chipper took his hand away, and Kristy looked at him sadly with just the hint of a smile. "You're pretty puffed up, but you don't have a black eye yet."

Chipper shook his head. "I guess we just stay here until they leave. What else can we do?"

The barrage began. Rodney and Benny collected about a dozen oranges each and took aim at the windows, throwing as hard as they could. Most of their throws missed, but occasionally some did pass through the window openings, and after a time, the inside walls were caked with a messy combination of juice, pulp and peel. They threw dirt clods and rocks, and it sprayed everywhere after it hit the outside or inside boards.

He and Kristy clung together in one corner. Both with bits of sticky orange in their hair and clothes. Powerless and humiliated. Eye hurting. He had to do something. He tried to lean over Kristy, protecting her. Their faces were pressed together, close enough to look into each other's eyes. Kristy's were hazel colored. For a few seconds, he forgot about Benny and Rod, concentrating on her face. She blinked when the dirt or orange sprayed inside. Orange peel was stuck in her hair, so he carefully picked it out. She smiled back.

Meanwhile, Rodney and Benny continued throwing. Kruger said, "Don't worry. They'll give up soon. Keep at it."

He peeked between the boards, seeing them below searching something to throw. There was Kruger inspecting a nearby tree. He reached for a rotten- looking orange lying beneath its branches. He bent over to grab it. Chipper was startled when an object sailed by Kruger's shoulder. It missed his head, and landed a few yards ahead, skimming along the ground

He turned to Benny, who was stooping over to pick up an orange from the ground, "Did you see that? Someone threw at me."

Before Benny could respond, a small, hard, orange whizzed toward him and hit squarely in the back of his neck. Benny grunted in surprise and whirled around to see where it came from. Kruger watched his friend get smacked and moved low behind the nearest tree. Benny hurried over and joined Rodney, both hunched over and searching the tree line in front of them.

Chipper tapped Kristy on the shoulder and pointed between the boards where he'd been watching. "Look at this."

Kristy leaned to look.

"There, can you see 'em?"

"Not really."

"Two rows. By those boards See him moving behind them?"

Rodney and Benny moved cautiously away from the tree house.

"Who's throwing at us?" asked Rodney.

"Not sure. They hit me. I'm gonna hit 'em back," answered Benny warily.

Rodney scanned the trees close by. He turned, yelling up at the tree house. "Chipper! I'm pissed now."

Through the partial opening in the trees Chipper saw a lanky, dark-haired boy circle behind Rodney and Benny. He moved quickly, and had oranges bulging out of his pockets.

With a fury, he attacked Rodney and Benny, throwing hard as he ran at them. Rodney was hit in the thigh. Benny dropped his oranges and ran for it down the nearest aisle of trees. Another orange hit Kruger, this time on the top of the head as he spun to follow his friend. The tall and agile boy ran past Rodney and threw again at Benny who was sprinting at full speed. The orange sailed over Benny's left shoulder, but a second throw caught him in the seat of the pants. This time Benny made no sound as he scampered away. Rodney Kruger raced in the opposite direction. The attacking boy turned, and like a pitcher throwing a fastball, flung his last two oranges over Rodney's head.

Chipper and Kristy stood and shouted, "Yes! Yes!"

Laughing, Kristy clapped her hands in relief. Chipper hurried to open the hatch door. The pain under his eye didn't matter now. He was pretty sure he knew who had run off Rodney and Benny. It must be Roger Bell.

CHAPTER 7

Roger Bell had few close friends and spent most of the time with his dog, Spike, running around exploring the groves and working on his parent's small citrus grove. His tree house in the rear of their property was the most spectacular anyone had ever seen. There was a swing that hung from a high branch and allowed you to jump out and away from the outer edge of the structure and swing in a huge arc toward the ground. Kids loved it. Chipper had always liked Roger, even though he didn't know him well. Two years older, he was entering high school in the fall.

Roger spent his time wandering the groves. He was the guy you wanted on your team in an orange fight. Kids in the groves threw oranges at each other for fun, but you didn't get into any kind of orange throwing contest with Roger. Roger pitched a fastball and was fearless.

Being hit by an orange didn't actually hurt much, but if Roger hit you, it did. It was rumored that he'd once done a hundred push-ups in P.E. class. He was a tough kid.

Roger ran up to the tree house perch and yelled to Kristy and Chipper. "I saw those dopes attacking your place. I could hear 'em yelling from way over there." He pointed in the distance. "Figured you needed some help. I thought I'd get in some target practice, plus those two are idiots. Hey, did you really build this yourself?"

Roger looked up at the plywood floor above his head. "Nice job! How long has it been here?"

"We just finished a few weeks ago," Chipper replied. "Doog and Craig helped too. Do you want to go inside?"

"Okay."

Chipper opened the hatch. Roger bounded through the hole in the floor and stood in the big square hut. Roger was taller than either Kristy or Chipper, but still had room for his head.

"Man! What a mess!" said Roger. "I guess Benny and Rod were throwing for awhile before I came."

"Yeah, for too long. We can clean up." Chipper replied.

Roger leaned out the windows on each side of the tree house. "Seems real sturdy. Pretty bitchin'. Where did you get this wood?"

"Mostly from Doog's uncle, he's a carpenter. Plus, we went around to some construction sites. His uncle gave us some two by fours he didn't need, and even hauled the stuff over to Doog's. We bought the nails with our own money."

"This is a perfect tree," said Roger. "It's old with thick limbs."

"When did you find this tree, Chipper?" asked Kristy.

"Craig knew it was here," answered Chipper. "It was mainly his idea to build it. We started a few weeks before summer vacation."

"I just hope Ramos doesn't find it," said Roger. "T.J. would probably tear it down. Hopefully, he won't pass through here for a while. At least it is hidden from view by the eucalyptus trees."

"You could ask Mr. Ramos if it's okay to have your tree house here. Maybe he would say yes," suggested Kristy.

Chipper said, "We could ask, but what would happen if he said no? Then we would lose it right away."

No one spoke. They had known the risk that Ramos might find the tree house. One day it would be discovered and perhaps even taken down, or wrecked by Benny and Rod, but there wasn't much to do about that.

Roger began working down the steps to the ground, followed by Kristy and Chipper, who placed the lock on the hatch door.

Roger said, "See ya." He disappeared back into the grove and away from the shade of the big tree.

Chipper and Kristy started walking back the way they had come.

"I should have asked Roger about Dirty Charlie."

"Who?"

"Oh, some guy Craig's brother talks about. Craig told us about him last night. He lives in the grove somewhere. Doog and Craig want to go searching for him."

"Good luck. Let me know if you find him." She frowned. "But, why would you want to?"

"I don't really. Not sure he's even real. I think Thomas is making it up."

"Doesn't sound good. Hope you're right." When they reached the sidewalk, Kristy spoke again. "I need to get cleaned up before Mom notices. My parents are always telling me to stay out of the groves."

"Yeah, me too."

"Thanks for taking me out there. I won't tell anyone"

"I know. What's my cheek look like?"

"Pretty red."

"It still hurts."

She touched Chipper gently below his bruise. "Hope it gets better. See you around."

"Thanks. See ya." Chipper turned toward his house and walked up the driveway where his father had parked the '62 Chevy Nova.

Hungry, he walked to the kitchen and opened the fridge. Nothing. Potato chips sound good. Opening the lower cabinet, he found a half empty sack. A handful and then he was on his way to his room. He stopped and listened. Mother was talking to his dad in the bedroom. How did her voice sound? He would notice even the slightest change. Especially in the afternoon. His father's voice. No anger or frustration, so he relaxed.

CHAPTER 8

Mid-June, temperatures in southern California were often in the eighties. Sometimes ninety degrees. Go to the beach, play in the sand and sea. Cool off in a swimming pool or a yard sprinkler.

Chipper hadn't seen Craig or Doog for a couple days. They didn't know about his run-in with Rodney and Benny. This morning his father had left him the usual list of chores, which Chipper finished right after breakfast. Later, it would be too hot. Out the front window he watched his mother drive away in her red convertible. Unusual, as she rarely drove the Chevy Bel Air. Mostly it sat parked in the garage.

It disappeared around the corner.

He'd get the tree house hatch key and then find his friends. Outside, looking down the block, there was Craig throwing a baseball with his oldest brother James and another friend. They were playing pickle.

As he approached the three, Craig nodded at Chipper saying in a low voice, "I guess your parents never found out, right?"

"Nobody knows, except Kristy. I told her."

"Why tell her?" Craig threw the ball back to James, who was trying to tag the base runner in the middle.

"I'll explain later." Chipper sat on the curb. He watched the three play the game for about ten minutes before James had another friend show up and the three retreated into the house.

"I heard Kruger is looking for you. I think he wants to beat you up," Craig said, laying down his mitt and approaching Chipper.

"Who said that!" said Chipper, surprised.

"Doog told me he heard that from a bunch of kids at the field." He was referring to the Little League playing field where he and Chipper were on a team.

Chipper shook his head. "Why is that guy so mad at me? I've never done anything to him. He and Benny started throwing oranges at Kristy and I at the tree fort. One of them hit me in the face. It's a mess there. I was go—"

"What happened at the tree house?" interrupted Craig.

Chipper told Craig about the orange attack days before.

When his story was done, Craig said, "Maybe he'll just forget all about it. A guy like Rodney has so many enemies he probably has a hard time keeping track of them."

"Yeah, well, just in case, let me know if you see 'em around. I don't want to get into a fight. He'd kill me."

Craig changed the subject. "Have you been back out there?"

"No."

"I haven't either. Maybe we should go clean it."

"Good idea. Let's see if we can find Doog."

Craig took his mitt and threw it on his porch. They started in the direction of Doog's house. Walking up the sidewalk, Doog's Mom's car approached them, with Doog in the passenger seat. She stopped beside Chipper and Craig and their friend got out asking, "What's up?"

"Do you want to go to the tree house?" Craig told Doog an abbreviated version of Chipper's run-in with Rodney and Benny.

"That's bad," was Doog's comment.

Chipper pointed at his cheek. "You can still see where I got hit in the face."

"Think they'll come back?" Doog asked.

"I guess we'll find out. I did lock it, though," said Chipper.

"Anyone got the key?" asked Craig.

Chipper showed his.

"Good, let's go." Craig hurried his pace toward the grove.

Amongst the orange trees it was cooler. The grove held few ripe oranges. The ground was soft and difficult to walk through. Chipper's feet nearly disappeared into the dusty earth with each step. After some time walking and talking about their worries with Rodney and Benny, Doog turned to Chipper. "I saw your mother at the store. Do your parents drink a lot of wine? Her whole shopping basket was filled with wine bottles."

Chipper's throat felt tight as he searched for an answer. "I don't think my parents even drink wine. It must be for someone else." He wondered if Doog would believe the lie. It was partly true. His dad didn't drink wine or beer, or any alcohol, for that matter. But, the wine part was true. He had lied before to protect himself. Doog seemed to accept the answer and the conversation changed.

Hot and tired, they arrived at the old avocado tree. The outside of the tree house showing the many orange and dirt stains. Inside was just as bad. Flies and gnats were everywhere. Globs of orange rind and dirt mixed together. The sweet smell of overripe orange.

"Looks pretty bad," said Craig. "All we can do is clean the inside the best we can."

Doog and Chipper started tossing out the smashed oranges. After some quick work, Craig spoke up, "It's better already."

Chipper and Doog nodded. Then Doog said, "You know...what about looking for Dirty Charlie?"

Dirty Charlie. What to say? He'd forgotten about him.

Craig spoke up, "Chipper doesn't believe the story. He thinks my brother made it up."

Chipper grimaced. "I don't know, maybe I changed my mind. I don't care if we go."

Craig opened his mouth to say something, but held back.

Would Craig back off?

Chipper continued, "Really. I don't care."

Doog interrupted the uneasiness between the two friends. "Come on, what are we waiting for? Let's go!"

Chapter 9

Stretched out behind the tree fort was a double row of eucalyptus. Behind the skinny trees, another grove. This section extended for miles. The familiar smell of eucalyptus mixed with the pungency of thousands of oranges. Chipper knew little about this part of the groves. Passing an empty barn-like structure he tossed a few oranges at the tin roof, listening for a sharp bang as they hit. A dirt road divided one orchard section from another. Between the rows of trees was an irrigation system. They stooped to drink the moving water splashing from the cement cistern.

"It can't be too far to the other side. We have all day, so even if it goes for a long way, let's see where this ends." Craig crouched to drink.

"Okay, let's keep going," said both Doog and Chipper.

With renewed energy, they picked up their pace at first, cutting in and out among the green trees. Now and again, someone would search a tree, grab a ripening orange, and lob it at one of the others. After some time, they slowed. The sun shone in their eyes, no shade, and dry mouths. Nothing in either direction, but more trees.

A sweating Doog stopped. "This grove never ends," he said, with his hands on his hips. "Look down the row. Like, it's endless." Indeed, as far as they could see were orange trees running in a long straight line.

"And how do we even know this is Dirty Charlie's grove?" Chipper said. "It could belong to Ramos still. There's no way to tell. Can he own this large of an orchard? I don't hear any traffic from here."

Craig walked to a patch of green sour grass, snapped off a long stem, and placed it in his mouth.

Chipper took a deep breath, tired, but he was unwilling to tell his friends he wanted to stop the search. Craig wouldn't quit. He'd talk Doog out of it too. So, Chipper said, "Come on, Doog, we're this far, we might as well go on."

"Chipper's right," added Craig. "Let's keep going. At least for twenty minutes or so."

Doog had little support. "Listen." he said, "I'm tired and thirsty. Why doesn't Chipper just ask Roger? He must know something. He could ask about Dirty Charlie. Right, Chipper?"

What to say? He had no real close ties with Roger. "I guess I could ask him next time I see him. The thing is, I don't really know him that well."

"But he must like you cause of what he did for you and Kristy," said Craig.

Chipper nodded. "Okay, I'll do it, but I just hope he doesn't think I'm the crazy one."

Craig frowned, but Chipper smiled back, showing he meant no harm.

"If he says anything, you can tell him I'm the one who's asking," said Craig.

"Don't worry, I will."

Chapter 10

Out of breath, Kristy ran to Chipper's front yard. "I have to talk to you."

Chipper looked up from the bicycle he was polishing in his driveway. It was late morning and another sunny, early summer day, but the last few days had been smoggy.

Kristy looked around to see if anyone was nearby.

A neighbor was watering with a hose across the street. Most of the windows in the front of Chipper's house were open.

"Roger was on our block today. He was searching for you."

"For me?" Chipper asked. "Why?"

"Yeah, he went to your house," continued Kristy. "When he found out you weren't home, he came down to see me. He told me to tell you he wants to talk to you about something."

Puzzled, he stopped what he was doing and stood up holding the can of chrome polish. "Did he say anything else?"

Kristy took another look around, stepped closer to Chipper, and said in a loud whisper, said, "He wants to show you something, I think. He said he will come to your house early in the morning. He was acting strange, as though he was afraid someone was listening or following him. He said everything in a real quiet voice. The last thing he told me was not to tell anyone about meeting with you."

Chipper responded in disbelief. "What does that mean? I can't believe he needs me for anything."

"Well, he does," said Kristy, "And when you get back tomorrow you'd better come and tell me what it's all about. You can trust me, I haven't told about your tree house and I won't say anything about Roger either."

Kristy wouldn't tell, but it made no sense. Was it something to do with the day Roger chased off Benny and Rodney?

Kristy pushed her hair out of her eyes, and walked away. "I've got to go now. I have dance lessons, but I'll see you tomorrow, right?"

There were other questions he wanted to ask, but felt too surprised to think straight. "Right," he said, "I'll see you after I talk to Roger."

Kristy ran toward her house and then he continued polishing the inside rim of his stingray bike. Disappointed Kristy had to leave, he tried to think of reasons why Roger would seek him out. Roger knew where he lived. Wouldn't have expected that.

He pondered Kristy's story. Roger was coming in the morning. No worry about Mom then. Problems were nearly always in late afternoon. She might be curious what the older boy wanted. The best idea was to meet him out front and catch Roger before he got to the door.

Mid-morning the next day, the sun was still low in the

sky, but it was warming up. Chipper wore Bermuda shorts and a t-shirt. He went out to the garage, opened the big door, and took out his bike. He decided to ride it up and down the street until Roger showed up. When he passed the Cabrerra house, he noticed the grass still needed mowing and wondered if Kristy planned on cutting it like she said. The Cabrerra's car was out front, so they must be home. He pedaled to the end of the street past Kristy's, Craig, and Doog's houses but saw no signs of his friends.

Turning the bike around, he saw Roger walking around the corner at the far end of the street and pedaled fast to meet him. Normally, Roger wore a red baseball cap and sometimes his dog was with him, but today there was no dog or cap. He had an unusually serious look on his face and when he saw Chipper on his bike he stopped and waited for him to approach.

Chipper waved and then rode his bike into his driveway and left the blue stingray with the banana seat parked in front of the garage. Running to where Roger waited, he asked, "You looking for me?"

Roger turned and headed back the way he came and replied, "I am."

Chipper followed in the bigger boy's footsteps as he headed down the street away from Chipper's house.

Roger suddenly announced, "We're going to a place out in the grove, near your tree house. I have something to show you. I'll explain everything once we get there."

With that, both boys walked faster. They crossed the road and vanished into the immense orchard. Roger moved swiftly, so Chipper jogged a few steps to keep up with him.

All was quiet except for the birds calling. Minutes later,

Roger said, "A week ago I was cutting across this section of trees on my way to the field. There is a big eucalyptus that blew down in the windstorm last fall, and it's leaning against some other trees. I've never tried climbing it, but I did last week because I'm guessing it's going to get cut up by the grove workers soon. I wanted to see how high I could get. Anyway, it was hard working through the branches, but I was able to climb most of the way to the top. From up there, I could see all over the whole orchard. I noticed someone a few rows over. At first I thought it was a worker or some kid, but then I saw he was carrying a brown canvas sack. He didn't see me. I watched until I lost sight of him and then I got off the tree and followed to see what he was doing. He didn't go far."

Roger stopped now in front of what looked like a dead orange tree. Unhealthy brown trees weren't unusual in the grove. They were sprinkled here and there. Roger stepped between the dead tree and a healthy one to its side. He stomped the ground, looking for something.

Chipper's heart was pounding. What was this about?

Roger's foot tramping continued a few seconds—until he hit a spot sounding very different from the others. Chipper tensed, wondering what was there. Roger knelt and sifted through the dirt. Finally he seemed to find what he was looking for. Dirty boards appeared where there should have been solid ground. To Chipper's amazement, Roger kicked away the boards, and a dark, deep hole appeared. Chipper moved closer and peered over the side. At the bottom lay a canvas sack.

"I followed him to here. That's the sack he had." Roger pointed at the hole. "He took some things from the hole and then placed them inside the sack."

Roger opened the bag so Chipper could look inside. Mostly, it was filled with small jewelry, watches, silverware, loose change, and to Chipper's amazement, a pair of leather shoes.

"I recognize those shoes," Chipper said. "Did I tell you about sleeping in the tree house? The next morning someone tried to get in. I saw their shoes and I swear, they're the same ones. Why are they in here with that other stuff?"

"Who knows?" said Roger. "Maybe he just wanted them for himself and took 'em. Has to be stolen. It's the only thing that makes sense. I've been here three times before and sometimes there's much more in the sack than now. He must sell it somehow. Nobody keeps their valuables in a hole in the middle of an orange grove. This is a thief's hiding place."

Chipper looked around. What if he should reappear? His uneasiness increased. "Hey, let's just go to a phone booth and call the police. They'll take care of things. Right?"

"Hold on. I could have called the cops a long time ago, but I didn't. I have my reasons. I want to find out more about this thief and then we'll call the police. But for now, don't tell anyone. I mean nobody. Promise?"

Chipper wasn't going to change Roger's mind so he asked the question most on his mind. "Okay, promise, but why did you tell me about this, Roger? What good am I?"

"It's the tree house and other stuff, too. When I saw you there the other day I knew then it could make things easier. I'm hoping you'll let me use it. And since I had to ask you, I figured you'd need to know what for. Also, now that you know, I'm going to need one other thing, too. I'll tell you more later. Right now my plan is to watch this hole for a few days. Long enough to find out a little more about the thief and after that, I don't know. Let's see what happens."

Keeping this thing a secret would be hard. Kristy would want to know about Roger. What was the other reason Roger needed him? Right now he wanted to get away from the hole. He felt like he was doing something wrong.

"Okay, Roger. I'll get you the key for the hatch but let's cover this back up and go. It's making me nervous."

Roger carefully placed the bag back inside the hole and returned the boards. Then as they were kicking dirt back on top of the boards to disguise the hole, a man shouted, "Hey, what are you boys up to?"

It was T. J. Ramos, the grove's owner. "Roger, you're not having an orange fight, are you? If you are, do it in your own grove."

Roger and Chipper moved away from the thief's cache. "We're coming home from the field, Mr. Ramos," he said. He changed the subject. Pointing to the dead tree near Ramos, he said, "What's wrong with that tree? Why do you think it died?"

"Could be it's just an old tree that caught a disease." Ramos approached the two boys. He looked at Roger while he spoke. "Or it might not have gotten enough water some- how. I'll dig it up pretty soon and plant a new tree. There's another tree like this in the next aisle. I guess I'll take care of them both at the same time."

Chipper studied the man he had slightly feared for many years. Ramos carried a shovel and wore a pair of old blue overalls splattered with mud from working on the irriga- tion system. T. J. Ramos didn't look like a friendly person, but when he spoke to Roger, his tone was of good humor.

The outstanding feature on his suntanned face was a large almost purple nose. Most of Chipper's friends kept clear of the grove men. A younger neighborhood kid once told Chipper he'd been caught by T. J. during an orange fight and the red-nosed man threatened to call the police on him. The boy's parents were asked to pay for oranges the kids pulled from the trees. The parents refused to pay, but promised their son would be punished and would stay out of the grove. Chipper knew the boy didn't keep that promise, but he always watched out for T. J. Ramos.

Roger moved well away from the partially covered hole and continued to talk with the older man. "Do you have any good stories to tell, Mr. Ramos? Anything unusual happening in the groves lately?"

"Not much, really," replied Ramos. "Had to run out a couple of grove bums yesterday. Not a big problem. Just passing through, I suspect. Somebody has been damming up some of my irrigation ditches. Probably kids. Last week, though, I did see someone I haven't seen in a while. I knew he lived some miles from here, but I'd almost forgotten about him."

"Who's that?" asked Roger.

"That old man, Ol' Dr. Charlie." I think his real name's Charlie Jordan. Dr. Charlie Jordan, I'm pretty sure."

Chipper looked at the Ramos in disbelief. "Do people sometimes call him Dirty Charlie?"

"I'm not sure," said Ramos. "He sometimes looks pretty dirty. You'd never know he is a wealthy man. He's always dressed in the same clothes, and I know he lives in an old farmhouse not too far away. He owns a bunch of orchards, you know. Some border my property. I hardly ever see him, he keeps to himself."

Roger broke in, "Once, a long time ago, he came to our house to talk to my dad about something. I remember wondering why my dad even knew a person who looked like he did. But, my dad talked to him like he was a friend. I'd forgot about it till just now."

Chipper wanted to hear more. "Did he commit a crime or go to jail? I heard he's dangerous."

Both T.J. and Roger laughed lightly.

Then Ramos spoke. "Son, the only story that is true, is that he is quite wealthy, and kinda eccentric. I have no idea where crazy stories like yours get started, but then he is an unusual character and people just can't leave that alone."

Chipper had more questions, but Ramos started off holding his shovel, walking down a nearby aisle. Waving goodbye, he told them to stay out of trouble.

CHAPTER 11

The same day, Chipper hastened to find Kristy. She'd want to know about Roger. He'd have to tell her something, but omit some details. Share enough to make her happy.

Approaching her home, he could see Kristy across the street mowing the Cabrerra's front lawn.

She was probably making a lot of money today.

Kristy caught sight of Chipper as he approached and waved for him to come across the street. Chipper nodded and went over.

"I'm almost through, wait for me." She turned the mower in the opposite direction.

"Okay," Chipper said in a loud voice.

Kristy mowed past him. Chipper walked to the curb and sat. Further away, Doog and his parents were getting into their car. The big Buick backed out of the driveway and cruised in his direction. Craig was in the back seat. Both boys leaned out the window toward Chipper and waved. Doog's mother honked lightly on the horn.

Chipper waved back. "Where are you going?" he yelled.

Doog leaned out further. "Going to the beach!"

Chipper waved again to let Doog know he heard. Their car halted at the stop sign at the end of the street, turned left and disappeared.

Doog's mom often took her family to the beach. It wasn't so easy at his house. Dad planned a picnic, but by the end of the day, Mom might start drinking. Then, nobody wanted to go. Sometimes his father would take his sister Sandy and Chipper to a burger restaurant, to get out of the house.

It hurt to see Craig and Doog having fun without him. They invited each other on small outings like the one today. Unless they needed another person, Chipper was left out.

He looked back to see Kristy turn off the mower and for a moment all was silent before she spoke. "Let me put this mower away and then I want to talk."

He stood up from the curb and walked with her to the Cabrerra's garage.

"I need to let Mrs. Cabrerra know I'm through. I'll be right back."

Chipper stood outside the garage while Kristy went to the front door. The garage was mostly empty. An old desk sat in one corner. On top of the desk's sun-damaged top was what appeared like an old thick book of some kind. He examined it closer. A coin collection book. Without opening it, he could tell it was bulging with many hundreds of different coins. There were several display cases with odd coins. Around the sides of the garage stood stacks of boxes. In one box on the floor lay a display case of Indian arrowheads.

He hadn't seen so many in one place before. The back door to the garage opened, and Mrs. Cabrerra appeared.

"Hi Chipper, did I hear a doorbell ring? Kristy is probably searching for me."

"Yes, Mrs. Cabrerra. I think she's at the front door."

Kristy appeared around the corner. Mrs. Cabrera reached inside a pocket and handed Kristy a ten-dollar bill for her work. "Thanks for your help, Kristy. Would you do me one favor?"

"Sure, what's that?" asked Kristy.

"Mr. Cabrerra and I will be out of town for two weeks. Would you look after the yard and do some watering while we're gone? I just planted a lot of flowers in pots out back."

Kristy agreed, and the two made plans to talk again. Chipper and Kristy started out of Cabrerra's garage.

Kristy smiled at Chipper. "She always pays me better than anyone else. I've got my fireworks money now."

Chipper smiled. "I never get ten dollars for mowing. Usually five. I spend it right away so don't forget to share with your friends."

"I really will, you know, lots of sparklers. I wanna find someone with firecrackers. Do you know where?"

"Not really."

Kristy wiped a small amount of sweat from her hairline. "It's getting hot. Let's go sit in front of my house under that big tree."

They walked across the street and found a place in the cool grass under the shade of a large sycamore in the middle of Kristy's front yard.

"So, Chipper, are you going to tell me about what happened with Roger this morning?"

"Listen," said Chipper, looking around, especially toward the windows of the house. "I can't tell anyone, nobody at all!"

"Yeah yeah, I know all that," said Kristy, annoyed. "Just tell me what he wanted, that's all."

Chipper told Kristy a few details. "Roger saw some guy bury things in the grove. So, I guess Roger wants to use the tree house while he spies on 'em. Wants to see what he's doing, I guess. I gave him a key. That's all I know now but you have to keep it to yourself. Don't tell Roger I told you. Don't tell anyone."

Kristy was quietly thinking while Chipper told the story. After a moment, she said, "That Roger's pretty brave. What if he gets caught watching him? Who knows what might happen?"

The uneasiness returned. "You're right but, he'd have to catch him first,"

"Roger's pretty good with an orange," said Kristy. "He could probably knock 'em out with one."

Both laughed thinking back on Roger's onslaught when he routed Benny and Rod.

In the distance came a shrill whistle, the sound his father made when it was time to come to dinner. It was a distinctive sound unlike any of the other whistles fathers used to call in their kids. Chipper said goodbye to Kristy and started down the street.

Had he told her too much? What if Roger does get caught? He turned around and yelled back to Kristy, "I think this whole thing is a bad idea. I hope Roger knows what he's doing."

Chapter 12

Amongst the orange trees, in the grove owned by T.J. Ramos, a single figure scampered ghostlike through the midnight darkness. A muffled clanking came from the canvas sack slung over his shoulder. He walked quickly, coyote-like, eyes straining to find landmarks. Never using his flashlight, he had walked this route many times before. The sights and sounds of the orchard at night were now familiar. Pausing, he searched ahead for the dead tree, until it appeared faintly in the distance. Unlike the dark green shapes that surrounded him all the way through the grove, the tree showed only dried up brown branches. He stepped between it and a healthier one and smiled.

"So easy," he said to himself.

Moving carefully, he unearthed the battered boards that hid his secret. Setting them aside, he took the canvas sack, and dropped it softly down in the black hole. After replacing the boards, he kicked dirt back over the top. He left no sign of his presence and disappeared into the mass of orange trees that hid him so well.

In Chipper's tree house, Roger Bell lay uncomfortably on a dusty Boy Scout sleeping bag he'd brought from the garage. It wasn't unusual for Roger to sleep in his own tree house during the summer. His parents believed he was there now. Fully awake, he looked at his watch. It was three a.m. He crawled out of the bag and climbed through the hatch door and down the tree. The moon cast a shadow as he moved through the orchard.

Approaching the area where the board-covered hole was located, he slowed, senses sharpened for any unusual sound or movement. Cautiously he approached the dead tree, but seeing no one, he uncovered the boards. The ground opened up. He reached into the blackness, felt the heavy sack and knew the stranger had made a visit that night. Before he went to sleep at the tree house, Roger had checked the hole. There was no sack, just a few items sitting at the bottom. That had been at ten-thirty. Roger replaced everything as it was. Now, he had a plan.

Chapter 13

Chipper hadn't seen Craig or Doog for two days.
Chipper's family drove to visit cousins who lived two hours
north, near Santa Barbara. It was a dull trip. Both the kids
his age were at summer camp already. Chipper spent the
majority of time with his sister or the adults.

The last time he visited, the twins, Michael and Eddie,
took him to an old barn at the end of a gravel road in a
lemon orchard. They amused themselves playing in and
around the rickety building all day. Under a tarp, they
found a vintage automobile with no wheels. They jumped
inside and pretended they were gangsters. That was nearly
two years ago.

Chipper and his sister went looking for the barn. It was
gone, and so was the orchard. In its place was a shopping
center and a huge parking lot. It was all new. All over the
black asphalt were brightly marked parking spaces, newly
painted. There was a grocer and a druggist and a liquor store
was wedged between them. Was this really where the barn
used to be? They entered the drug store and searched for
the comic book section. While his sister looked at records

he leafed through a Batman comic before buying a Nestles Crunch Bar. Bored, they returned to his cousin's house.

Arriving home, Doog and Craig were playing with a baseball near the end of the street. He retrieved his mitt and ran to join them. He liked playing pickle. With faster reactions than either Doog or Craig, he excelled at this game.

"Where you been?" asked Doog.

"Friends of my parents."

"Have fun?"

"Not really. Their kids weren't home. Not much to do."

He ducked under a late tag from Craig. "Out!" said Craig.

"No way. I had the base before you got me."

Craig didn't argue and threw the ball back to Doog. Chipper took a lead off. Doog faked a throw and Chipper started to run towards the safety of the base. Doog smiled, knowing he'd fooled him and rushed to put on the tag. Chipper couldn't turn fast enough and Doog had him. But, at the last second, Chipper went low to the ground and Doog's momentum pushed him past the prone Chipper who crawled on his hands and knees toward the base. Doog turned to tag him, but laughed at his own mistake. "Crap! I always fall for that. Damn, you're quick!"

Sweaty and hot after thirty minutes, they rested in a shaded spot on Doog's front lawn.

"I think you're the best at pickle, Chipper," Doog said. "You playing Pony League next year?"

"Yeah, I think so," Chipper answered. "I wanna make All-Stars this year. I'm a pretty good fielder, but I wish I hit better."

"You're good, Chipper," added Craig. "You started at

second base for three years in a row. Nobody ever starts for three years."

Chipper smiled, He did well in baseball, especially fielding at second base. He made Jr. All-Stars two years in a row and this year the goal was the league All-Star team. It was the only sport Chipper was better at. In football and basketball, both Craig and Doog excelled.

He changed the subject. "Hey, did I tell you...the other day, I found out about Dirty Charlie."

"Really!" Craig eyed Chipper. "Did you talk to Roger?"

"What did he say?" Chimed in Doog.

"Yeah, I saw him. A couple days ago. He was cutting through the grove, and came out near the end of our street."

He'd have to lie a little bit.

"Actually, I found out everything from listening to the Grove Man. He came up and started talking to Roger when I was there. I asked about Dirty Charlie and he said he'd seen Dirty Charlie last week. I guess he really is rich and everything. He looks like a bum or hermit or something like that. He owns a bunch of land around here and was once a doctor. I don't think the stuff about the mental hospital and all that is true though. He isn't a criminal."

"But, most of it is true huh?" said Craig, listening closely.

"I guess so," answered Chipper, shrugging.

"Did he say where he lives?" asked Doog. "Did you find out what's behind our tree house?"

"Not really," said Chipper. "I didn't want to bring up anything about the tree house to the Grove Man."

"I betcha he lives in that big orchard we explored before. We should try looking again," suggested Craig.

"How about tonight after dinner, when it's cooler"? said

Doog. "I sorta remember where we ended our search before. We just need to keep going this time."

They agreed to meet back at Doog's after dinner. Vowing to go all the way to the end of the bigger grove that bordered the long line of eucalyptus near their tree house, they split up for home.

In the hour after dinner, the sun was low in the sky and the temperatures were cooler. Craig and Chipper waited at the corner for Doog to show up. Before long he emerged from his house part way down the block. Within seconds, he joined them, and the three jogged toward the line of eucalyptus and then into the first row of fruit trees.

Chipper suggested going to their tree house first to check on it. Once there, they asked Chipper if he had the key to the latch lock, which he didn't. In fact, he had loaned the only key he had to Roger. Doog had a key too, but it was at home.

"We should hide a key around here somewhere so we don't have to keep remembering to bring it," suggested Craig.

"Good idea," agreed Doog. "I'll try to remember to bring mine, and then we can find a good hiding place. I'm going to check the hatch door though. See if it's locked."

He scrambled up the wooden steps, stepped out on the large limb just below the floor of the tree house, and looked up. The lock was in place. Doog peered through the cracks in the floor.

"I can kinda see some big blanket or something in there. Did we leave stuff here? I don't remember that. I think I see a pillow too."

Of course. Roger had left something to sleep on. Maybe

a blanket to keep warm while he waited at night. Roger had gone ahead with his plan. What to say?

Craig looked at Chipper. "None of my stuff is in there. Did you leave anything?"

Chipper pretended to think about Craig's question; he knew he hadn't. There was no legitimate reason for anything to be inside. He shrugged and shot them a perplexed look.

Doog started to climb down, jumping to the ground from the third step. "I guess we'll find out once we get the key. Seems weird, though."

"There is no way to get inside, so it must be our stuff," Chipper replied.

After visiting the tree house, they walked back beyond the shade of the avocado tree and through a thick line of eucalyptus, the thin bark crunching under their feet as they went. Past the row of eucalyptus, Doog grabbed a handful of yellow and green sour grass and bit into the tart stem. He grimaced at the sour taste, but then took another bite. Craig stood looking up and down the long rows of short stumpy orange trees.

"I think T.J.'s grove ends here."

There was a difference in the ground. The first orchard had been plowed recently and was soft, the brown dirt easily finding a way into the sides of one's shoe. The new grove had hard, compacted dirt, left unplowed. There were irrigation channels where they drank water the last time. Chipper saw an old rusting sign at their feet and turned it over. The other side read, "Private Property. No Trespassing."

"I've never seen a sign before," said Craig. "The Grove Man doesn't use them."

Shortly, the boys came to the spot where they thought

they stopped previously. There was a plum tree, which seemed out of place, but Doog said he remembered it from before. They pushed on past the tree of unripe plums and continued further into the orchard. It was difficult to get a bearing as taller trees loomed in every direction. They stopped to get more sour grass, which they chomped as they walked.

Craig was in the lead when he halted and pointed at a rustic building about hundred feet ahead. "Whose house do you think that is?"

Doog answered, "It's only a shack, not really a house."

Chipper doubted whether anyone lived there. "That's not a house. It looks like a storage building maybe. Is there a house on the other side?"

Doog picked up an orange and threw at the side of the metal building. It struck with a loud bang.

Craig and Chipper ducked. "What are you doing?" Craig yelled at Doog.

Doog dropped the other orange he held. "Sorry. Just wanted to see if I could hit the side from here."

The three crept closer to the ramshackle building. The surrounding silence was abruptly broken by the barking of a dog. The deep bark came from behind the old shed. Chipper searched the ground in that direction, hoping not to see any movement. Doog and Craig froze in place.

"Crap." Doog stepped back. "It's a guard dog."

Startled, Chipper retraced his steps. Could he climb up a tree before the dog came around the corner?

Craig remained where he had stood, tiptoeing to see inside a window of the shack. He turned and pleaded with his friends, "Don't go yet. Just wait."

The dog's barking was closer. Chipper had visions of a Doberman Pinscher suddenly appearing before them.

He jumped when a man called, "What are you boys doing!"

He didn't wait to see who was talking. He dropped the sour grass and sprinted from the shed where Craig stood stark-still. A glance over his shoulder, and there was a man approaching Craig. Their friend appeared unable to move.

Chipper sped up, running into the welcome maze of the grove. Repetitive barking continued behind him. Was he being chased? On the next aisle, Doog was already ahead of him, zigzagging between the trees. Chipper cut in and out of the rows trying to keep pace.

Don't lose track of Doog. Was Craig running with them too? There was only Doog, but he was getting further ahead. Chipper turned and ran down the next row. No Doog. Stop and look for him. Daring to look back over his shoulder, he almost expected to see a dog, teeth bared.

He ducked under the low canopy of one of the orange trees. Trying to catch his breath, sweat dripped down his forehead, He was shaking. What now? No sounds, but still a dog barked in the distance.

A quick rest, and then which direction is home? Down one long aisle, a grove worker stood shovel in-hand. The tall, dark skinned worker in a wide brimmed hat turned and peered in Chipper's direction. Was the worker yelling something? Need to get going, shouldn't have stopped.

There was automobile traffic, a horn honked and a sound of a noisy vehicle, maybe a garbage truck. A slow jog, still wary, but were those moving cars which meant a road. Minutes later scampering, he burst out of the grove onto what he recognized as Fourth Street. A half hour walk and he'd be back in his own neighborhood.

Not far from his house, and across the street from the grove, a blue postal mailbox made for a handy place to wait and watch. Chipper boosted himself atop the metal perch. Surveying the grove in both directions, were Doog and Craig already ahead of him at home? Street traffic passed, but nobody came out of the grove. Finally, far down the street Doog moved cautiously out of the edge of the orchard.

Chipper yelled, "Doog!"

Doog ran to where he was sitting atop the mailbox. In a hurried voice he blurted, "Have you seen Craig? I've never run so fast. That dog! Was he chasing us? How long have you been here?"

"For a while. I came out way over on Fourth. You didn't see Craig?"

"No! This is bad! I don't think he got away. What should we do now?"

Chipper hesitated. "Don't know, but we better wait and see if he comes out. Should we go back and look for him?"

"It's getting too late." said Doog motioning west, where the sun was setting. "By the time we got back there, it would be dark."

In the dimming light they scanned the street hoping to see Craig emerge from the tree line. Time passed. The streetlights were close to turning on.

Two cars cruised past and then a white Ford truck, commonly used by workers in the orchards. A truck passed just in time to see Craig sitting in the front seat of the cab. Craig frowned and nodded at Chipper as he passed.

Chipper pointed down the road at the vehicle. "Did you

see that? Craig was in that white truck!"

"Are you kidding? No way!" said Doog,

"Really, he was!"

Cautiously walking in the direction of the truck, Chipper wondered aloud, "Is he turning down our street?"

"Crap, he is," said Doog as the white Ford slowed to turn. Running to the corner, the truck turned into Craig's driveway. The driver got out of the truck and walked up to the front door with Craig following.

CHAPTER 14

At midnight, he studied the locked house. For weeks he'd noticed that late evenings, nobody was ever home. Two nights ago, he'd even knocked on the front door. The windows were locked; there was no easy access. He checked the door that led in from the backyard. The door was bolted. Next, in the shadows, he came to the window that looked inside the garage. It slid open. With the canvas sack, he entered the window.

Inside, the flashlight came on searching for an entrance into the house. He lit up a corner of the room where two short steps led to a door. He tried the knob. Locked. He could smash it open if he had to. He had a small crowbar in his back pocket along with a set of tools. He shined the light around the garage looking for anything of value. There was an old dusty desk with a big thick book on top. He noticed a coin collection and placed it in the bag. Nearby were several more cases that contained coins. He grabbed them all. He pointed the light inside one box and saw an arrowhead collection. He took it. Around the dark interior of the garage, the flashlight beam bounced off the wooden rafters.

Outside the garage, there were voices. First one, and then another. Two people talking, on a late night walk. He clicked off the flashlight. The voices came closer—a man and a woman—and grew dimmer as the two passed the house. Another moment, silence again. He moved to the door. From his pocket, he pulled the small set of tools. He started to pry the door open. The ring of a telephone just inside the door startled him; he dropped the big screwdriver and fell back from the door for a moment.

The phone continued ringing. The man was sure no one would answer. He was positive the house was empty. But when the ringing stopped, his hands trembled. He'd found stuff of value in the garage. He hesitated and backed down the two steps, he picked up his tools and backtracked to the open window. From ceiling to floor the flashlight shone round one more time, just in case he'd missed anything. The usual garage items, lawnmower, two pails, shovels, rakes, old paint and a workbench.

Out through the window and into the nighttime back-yard. Momentarily, a light from the neighbor's back porch lit up the robber. A nylon stocking hid his face. The thief ran for the back fence, and worked his way over the top. Behind the house another orchard bordered the neighborhood. Deftly, he blended into the shadows of the grove.

CHAPTER 15

The yellow wall phone rang twice before his mother answered. Concentrating on the tone of her voice, he guessed she hadn't been drinking yet. Whoever was calling did the most talking. His mother spoke briefly, thanking someone, and then hung up. Chipper waited for his name to be called and it was.

He worried the phone call had to do with the previous day's events. He'd wondered last night if there'd be a call, especially from Craig's parents. Now Mom wanted to talk to him. Had to be about Craig. What to say. What had Craig told his parents?

His mother stood washing dishes at the sink, her back to Chipper. "That was Craig's mother."

"Yeah."

"An orchard worker brought him home last evening. The man said that he'd ignored the no trespassing signs and was throwing oranges at a building. He also said two other boys ran off. Were you one of them?"

"Yeah, but I didn't throw anything. I ran 'cause there was this dog. It was barking, growling and stuff."

"Why were you in that grove? It's not near here. I don't like you wandering around any groves."

"Craig wanted to look for Dirty Charlie. He still believes that story and I went along."

"I thought we already talked about that."

"I know, but Craig still wants to look and talked Doog into it."

"Hmm, okay, but no more going to that grove, and pay attention to trespassing signs. He could have called the police. And, don't do everything Craig suggests. Use your own brain."

"Yeah, Mom. I will. Can I go now?"

"Go do your chores. Dad left a list for you. Stay out of the groves. Find something else to do."

"Okay, I will."

Mom was pretty nice in the morning. If it had been afternoon when Craig's Mom called, what then? Good thing it was Craig who was caught. What would it be like if the grove worker dragged him to the front door? Need to find out from Doog about Craig.

The chores were few, and in an hour he was done. There was Doog to see, and Kristy, too. In two days it would be the Fourth of July. Kristy. Maybe she would walk with him to the fireworks stand in the parking lot near the supermarket. How much money did he have? He looked in his top dresser drawer. A couple dollars, but it was always fun to see the fireworks for sale.

His mother started out the front door and told Chipper she was going to the grocery store. Was that true? He didn't want to think about it. She was probably going to the liquor store. Why was it this way? The same thing over and over.

Dad never talked about it. Neither did Chipper. None of his friends knew. He never spoke to his sister. Never talked to anyone.

Would it stop someday? How far back he could hardly remember. Second grade. That bad day when he was home sick. That time, she started drinking in the morning. He called Dad. Dad came home, but then he left for work again. It was like Dad pretended nothing was wrong. But, he knew.

Gotta see Kristy first. Another hot afternoon and it was smoggy. The brown haze hung on the trees in the distance. He walked to the front porch and knocked, but it looked like nobody was home. There wasn't a car in the driveway and all the curtains were closed. He rang the doorbell a few times. No answer.

Go to Doog's then. Looking across the street, it appeared the Cabrerra's were still away. Chipper remembered the conversation Kristy had about watering for them. She probably wouldn't be gone too long. Hopefully, Doog was home.

Doog was on the side of his house painting a short picket fence. The white paint dripped from his brush and he had splotches of paint on his hands and face.

"Hey, Chipper," Doog said. "Did you get in trouble?"

"Some."

"Me, too. I have to paint this whole fence before I get to leave the yard. It's going to take forever."

"Have you seen Craig?" Chipper sat on the shaded grass.

"Just once. He was in his parents' car. I saw him drive by. I'll bet he's really in hot water. I know his mother doesn't like him hanging out in any groves. I think she'll ground him for a long time. She's strict."

"Yeah. Much stricter than my parents. I was told never

to set foot in that orchard again. Just my Mom knows. She'll tell my dad and then he'll say something, too. But, my dad told me when he was a kid he played in the groves all the time.

Who was that guy, anyway? Was he the owner, or just a worker? I know he wasn't Dirty Charlie. He wasn't old enough."

Doug shook his head. "I don't know, but I'm never going near there again!"

Chipper looked over at Craig's house. There was no sign of Craig. No reason to be mad at Craig for telling on Doog and him. The man saw the other two boys. He probably asked Craig who they were.

Looking back at Doog, he said, "Maybe you'll be finished tomorrow if you work on the fence all day."

"Yeah, hopefully."

"Well, anyway, come get me when you're done."

"Yeah, right. See ya."

He turned to walk back out to the sidewalk. Might be a boring day. Maybe Kristy will come home later.

Ahead, someone in the distance was approaching on the sidewalk. It was Rodney Kruger. Chipper turned back around. Had Rodney spotted him? His heart pounded as he reached Doog's driveway, and then sprinted the rest of the way to where Doog was painting.

"What's the matter?" Doog set down his paintbrush.

Chipper ducked behind a bush next to the house. He blurted, "Kruger's coming down the street. What should I do?"

"Oh geez!" Doog jumped up. "Stay there. Let me look." Doog walked toward the front of his yard. As he neared the corner of the house, he stopped and then cautiously continued.

From where he sat, Chipper couldn't see anyone at all on the sidewalk. Three more steps and Doog emerged onto the front lawn. No Rodney.

"He's gone, Chip. I don't see him anywhere." Doog kept peering up the street.

"You sure?" He emerged from behind the bush.

Doog twisted back in his direction. "Get back! Get back!!" he hissed.

Chipper bounded behind the bush again.

Doog rushed to join him. "He was at Kristy's front porch. I didn't see him, but now he's headed this way."

Was there an escape? A fence enclosed the side of the house. How hard would it be to jump it? Probably too late. Had Rodney seen Doog?

"Crap, he'll see us," Doog whispered in Chipper's ear, as the two pressed close to the house.

Through the filter of the bush, Chipper saw Kruger striding by. Did he just look over at them? Chipper closed his eyes, then opened them soon enough to see him clearly: red hair, freckles, and the tough look. Rodney never wore shorts, even in summer. Always jeans, and a pair of dirty boots.

Kruger disappeared past the next house. Chipper started breathing again. Less tense, they warily peeked around the neighbor's house in time to see the older boy disappear down the street.

Puzzling. What would Kruger be doing at Kristy's door? Maybe she would know. Still, it didn't make sense.

CHAPTER 16

As the Fourth of July approached, Roger Bell came to see Chipper. Since meeting with him at the dead tree, Chipper hadn't seen or heard anything from Roger. Maybe Roger changed his plans, perhaps left town on a vacation with his parents.

But through the window there was Roger waving and yelling, "Come out."

Chipper went to meet him at the front door. Chipper's mother was in her room. That was good. She'd likely question what the older boy wanted with Chipper. He took no chances. Before Roger could get to the door, Chipper opened it and whirled past him, walking towards the sidewalk.

"Let's go to the tree house," he urged.

Roger nodded, and they walked side by side down the street towards the grove. "I need you to do a few things for me," Roger said, as they passed through the first row of trees.

"Anything you need, Roger, I'll try to help."

"That's good, because I need someone to help with my plans. I can't do it by myself."

It was surprising to hear that. What was Roger up to? Chipper didn't respond at first. Walking through the uneven ground, warmed by the summer's heat, he asked, "So, what do I do?"

"It's kinda complicated."

"Oh yeah. What part?"

"Really everything."

"Yeah."

"I might need your help tonight." Roger waited for Chipper's reaction. With no response, Roger continued, "I need you to meet me tonight after dark out here at your tree house."

Tense, Chipper took a deep breath. "What do you need me for? What would I do?"

"It's more like needing someone to vouch for me, a witness…something like that."

He gave Roger a confused look. When they reached the avocado tree, he grabbed the key from the hiding spot, and started up the two by four wooden rungs that were nailed to the base of the tree.

Roger had stashed an old wool sleeping bag and a small pillow in the corner. Chipper went to stand by one of the windows. "I don't get it, Roger. Witness for what?"

"I'm serious, Chipper, I need you for a reliable witness. Someone who hasn't been in trouble. You never been in big trouble, right?"

"But people would believe you, too, Roger, you're honest. What's the matter?"

"The problem is that I haven't always been the most trustworthy person. I've made some big mistakes. One real big one."

What a puzzle. Was there a way out of this? Be part of the plan. He'd wanted to use the tree house. But now...

Looking out across the grove and then at Roger. An ice cream truck chimed in the distance. It was slowly making its way up a nearby street. Hot—a popsicle would taste good right now. There was a quarter in his pocket. Enough to buy a fudge bar. Too far away though.

For a time it was quiet and then Roger spoke again. "See, I need someone like you being here when this whole thing happens, because the police might not consider me a good source."

"Why not?"

"They might not, that's all," Roger said, a little gruffly.

No one spoke. Would Roger tell him why? He started to ask, again, but Roger cut him off.

"My big mistake happened last summer. Remember the snack stand at the baseball field that was broken into and robbed? That was me. I did it. I'm not sure why. It was a challenge, I guess. I thought I could do it, and then one night I did. Once I got inside, I wasn't really sure if I even wanted to steal anything. I grabbed some boxes of candy, a little cash, and a radio and ran off with them. I kept it up in my tree house for a few days and then I started feeling guilty. I made a second mistake. I took the stuff back to the snack bar one afternoon and told them I found it. Someone called the police. Once the police came and started to question me, I just told the truth. I thought they'd let me go after I apologized and stuff, but I was put in the back of a police car and taken to some kind of room where they kept me until my parents came. The whole thing was so bad. My parents know a few policemen, and they were embarrassed and really angry. I was grounded the rest of the summer.

"The whole time since then I've wanted to prove to those cops and my parents that I'm not a liar or a thief and somehow make up for what I did. That's why I want to help get this robber arrested. But, if this goes wrong, I'll need someone like you to back up my story. Do you see what I mean?"

Chipper slowly dropped to the floor of the tree house and leaned back against the plywood sides.

Surprised Roger would tell him such a personal story, for a moment, he said nothing. The snack bar break-in. That was Roger. He'd forgotten about it. Everyone wondered who'd done it. "Yes, I see what you mean," he said finally. "But what is it you want me to do tonight? Like, what can I do?"

"Now listen," said Roger, suddenly turning toward him. "This is my idea. I'm sure it will work. I've thought it over and over. I've figured some of the thief's habits. He seems to come to the grove with the goods he's stolen right around midnight. I came and waited for him every night starting at three-thirty in the morning. Then, I came a half hour earlier until two nights ago. I finally was there when he came, which was around Twelve-thirty. Then last night, it was twelve-fifteen. I'd bet anything that on the nights he brings his bag of stolen stuff out to the hole, he will do it right between twelve and one."

Roger became more animated as he talked. "Soon. In fact, the next time we spot him with the loot in the grove, we'll call the police. He comes from the same direction every time. He walks practically under that big fallen eucalyptus tree. You know the one. That's where we'll wait, and then while you follow him to the dead tree, I'll run and call the police. They must have a bunch of robberies they're trying to solve. They will have to believe me and come to meet me. I'll try to get them out to the hole quick. But see, if for some reason we're late, I will need you there to back up my story. It would look pretty bad if the guy was gone and here I was again with stolen stuff. They'd probably just figure I was to blame. I want to show everybody, especially my parents, I meant what I said last year."

Roger sat back down, and Chipper could tell he was done. "There is one big problem, Roger. In the end, my parents would find out that I snuck out of the house and spent the night in the grove. They'd kill me!"

"You sure? Remember, you'll be responsible for helping catch a crook. Maybe be a hero." He looked at Chipper.

"Yeah, well. You say I only have to help you out if the crook guy isn't there when the police show up. I just tell 'em about the stuff in the ground and that you're telling the truth. Right? If they catch him, then I just go back home right? Nobody knows?

"Yes. That's it exactly.

Chipper looked down and then at Roger. The friendship bond between them had grown unexpectedly. If he said yes, he'd probably always be able to count on Roger. Even if Roger had stolen once, he seemed trustworthy. It was a huge risk though. What would his parents do if they got a call from the police in the middle of the night? Can't think about that. Does Roger know what he's doing? It seems like it, but…

"When do we start if I say yes?" Chipper asked.

"We'll try tonight. If he comes, it'll be a practice run. I'm a little worried about getting to the phone booth quickly when it's dark out. There's one at the baseball field. It's the closest. I've gotta remember to have a dime for the phone. Plus, we need flashlights. Can you bring one?"

Chipper nodded, as he thought through what Roger said.

"C'mon Chipper, we can do this!" Roger said, emphatically.

He looked at Roger's hopeful face. "Okay, yes, I'll help."

Chapter 17

In the afternoon Chipper walked down the street
to Kristy's. Did she still plan to buy a bunch of sparklers for
the Fourth of July? Her mother answered the door and told
Chipper to try again tomorrow. Kristy was staying an extra
day with friends they'd been visiting in San Diego. Chipper
said thank you, and left.

Walking home, a police car turned onto the street
and parked in front of Kristy's house. Police cars were an
uncommon sight on his short block. The uniformed officer
walked to the front porch and then someone opened the
door and he went inside. Maybe he's a friend. Were Kristy's
parents expecting him? Have to ask Kristy about that. He
turned back toward home.

Maybe later he'd search out Craig or Doog but not now.
He made his way to his room and sat on the bed, his eyes
scanning a comic book he'd already read. Closing it, he lay
face down. His head hung over the side; he stared at the floor.
Summer was more complicated than it had been just a few
weeks ago. Was he making the right decision with Roger?
He picked up his comic book again and started reading.

Minutes later, the door to his bedroom opened, and his mother poked her head in, "Your dad's working late tonight. There is some leftover chicken in the fridge and I'll make some mashed potatoes, too." She was stammering and stuttering.

It depressed him and he answered with a nearly inaudible, "Yeah, okay."

How could this happen so quickly? She looked so content and at peace just minutes before, when he entered the house. Now the confused, disoriented and child-like mother appeared, and it would stay that way until bedtime. She must've been drinking. It never took long. He should've found the bottle and thrown it out like he'd done in the past. A confused talk about something Chipper didn't understand ended and she closed the door.

He took a deep breath and dropped the comic. He felt anxious. Meeting Roger late tonight at the tree house. Dad not coming home. Now, Mom had been drinking. Too many bad things could happen. His mother might go visit the neighbor's, or get in the car. She might pass-out in bed. Actually, that could be good. Made things easier.

It was already past dinnertime when he ventured out of his bedroom. He could hear his mother talking on the phone, her muffled voice coming from his parent's bedroom. His sister was watching television. In the kitchen there was a pot of cooking potatoes on the stove. The water had evaporated off and the potatoes were starting to burn. He turned off the stove. Inside the refrigerator there was no leftover chicken. His dad had barbecued it a few days before. Not surprising the chicken was gone by now. He walked back towards his parent's room to see if he could hear to whom his mother was speaking. Did the person on the other end notice the slurred speech? It sounded like his mother was talking to her sister who lived in the Midwest. That happened a lot. She made long distance calls when his father was away in the evening.

Chipper went into the living room and joined his sister watching television.

At seven o'clock, the phone rang. Chipper ran to the telephone on the kitchen wall. He answered it at the same time as his mother on the bedroom phone. Her sloppy voice asking who was calling. It was Roger. Chipper cut in, "I've got it, Mom."

"Who is this?" his mother repeated.

"It's Roger, Mom." Chipper hoped she'd hang up. She didn't.

"Who is Roger?" she said in words so slurred Chipper was sure Roger must notice.

"He's a friend. Can you hang up now?"

The phone clicked and Roger started speaking. "You're still meeting me tonight, aren't you?"

Chipper pulled the cord around the corner away from where his sister sat. "Yes, I can be there. What time?"

"Can you get there by eleven?"

"Yes, I think so. If I am not there, just wait. My dad might be home late tonight. He should be home by eleven though. Also, I need to tell you something. There was a police car at Kristy's house today. A policeman went to the front door, and I think he talked to Kristy's mom or dad."

"Really!" Could you tell what they were talking about?"

"No, they went inside. I'll see Kristy tomorrow for sure, and I'll ask her."

His mother approached through the utility room door adjacent to the kitchen. He should get off the phone. Seeing her walk into the room, Chipper said quickly, "I've got to go. I'll see you later."

"Okay, but try to be on time, right?"

Chipper said, "Yes," and then swiftly hung up.

His mother grabbed the pot that held the boiled potatoes and started looking for a bowl to pour them into. She had a hard time holding onto the potatoes and locating the bowl at the same time.

Chipper reached in a cupboard and pulled out a large yellow bowl and placed it on the counter. "Here, I can do that."

She tried plopping the potatoes into the bowl, but two of them fell to the floor. She picked them up and placed them into the bowl with the others.

"What are you doing! Those just fell on the floor!"

"They're fine," his mother drawled.

"Let me do this." Chipper pulled the yellow bowl away.

"I can do it. Get the electric mixer for me."

While searching for the mixer, the doorbell rang.

His sister yelled, "I'll get it."

Chipper couldn't see the front door from where he was standing, but Doog's voice asked, "Is Chipper home?"

Chipper looked at his mother and realized she was still trying to find the mixer. He didn't know where it was either. He left her and walked to the front door.

Doog smiled. "Wanna come out?"

Chipper hesitated. He'd like to leave the house until his dad got home, but knew he should stay. "I haven't eaten yet, maybe after I'm done."

It was a lie, but he had to close the door on Doog before his mother wandered toward the front of the house.

"Okay, maybe see you later, then." Doog walked away from the porch. But, then he turned and asked Chipper about Craig.

Chipper thought about stepping out with Doog and closing the door, but in the background his mother kept asking about the mixer.

"I don't know anything new." He brushed off Doog's question and started to close the door.

Doog shrugged, said something Chipper didn't understand, and left. He closed the door and walked back to the kitchen. His mother hadn't found the mixer and was now slumped over making her way back into her bedroom. The door closed with a bang.

Relieved, he placed the potatoes in the refrigerator. While there, he pulled out some hot dogs, boiled some water, cooked the wieners, and placed them between some bread. Adding potato chips, he took his meal out to watch television.

Three hours later, Chipper was back in his room getting ready for bed. Why wasn't his father home yet? No phone call. What to do if he wasn't home by eleven? No problems with Mom so far. That was good. Lucky that she hadn't come out of her room at all. The house was quiet.

He kept his clothes on and lay back on his bed. On the nightstand was a small clock that showed ten after ten. A car was coming toward his street. Most of the cars passed by, but occasionally one slowed and then made the turn down the street. Headlights lit his window momentarily as the vehicle passed. When his father's car made that turn down the block, he'd know it, having memorized the sound. It was somehow different than all the other cars.

Without warning, a thud and another loud sound came from the kitchen. It was his mother. Tense now, he took a deep breath and all of his senses sprang to life. He opened his eyes and concentrated on the direction of the sound. His mother was loudly talking to herself. He got up and walked to his closed bedroom door. Should he intervene? The nightstand clock said 10:20. Where was Dad? He had to get going and meet Roger. Impossible right now. He opened the bedroom door and peeked out. The kitchen light was on. No sounds though. She must have returned to her bedroom. He turned and crept back to his room. About to climb into bed, he stopped and listened to the sound of a vehicle making its way toward his street. He waited to hear if it was slowing to turn. It did. Chipper looked hopefully towards his bedroom window. Was the car slowing? Yes. Outside, bright lights lit the garage door. His dad was home.

Thirty-five minutes later, he was outside trying to replace the screen to his bedroom window. It was so dark he couldn't see what he was doing, so he left it leaning against the house. He'd waited thirty minutes after his father arrived, but he'd probably be late meeting Roger.

Exiting the yard, Chipper dashed down the sidewalk straight into the grove. In the stress of the evening he'd forgotten the flashlight. There was no moonlight to help navigate his way to the tree house. Don't have to worry about finding the tree house. That was easy. What about bumping into the thief? He strained his eyes to see ahead and listened for sounds of someone walking nearby. He could run faster if it wasn't so dark. One left turn ahead, down a few rows, and he'd be there.

Finally, he arrived at the base of the old avocado tree. Chipper thought he heard someone nearby, the faint sound of feet moving along dirt. He stopped and turned his head in the direction of the sound. It is must be Roger. After a minute, it grew silent again. Underneath the tree house he whispered, "Hey Roger. You up there?"

No response. Again. "Roger!"

Nothing. He tried finding the key to the hatch, which was under some leaves near the base of the tree. Too dark. He started up the steps of the tree leading to the door in the floor. The lock was missing and the hatch was pushed open. Hesitation. The inside of the tree house was even darker than it was outside. He lifted his head up through the hatch and called Roger's name. There was something in one of the corners. Reaching over, he touched the fabric of what he assumed was a sleeping bag Roger was using.

Have to sit and wait. He leaned against the wall with his knees pulled tight to his chest. Those night sounds again like last time, plus some automobiles in the distance behind him. Had Roger already come and gone, because he was late? Should he keep waiting or walk back home? If he waited, for how long? He decided to shut the hatch door. The bang it made closing made him wince. It sounded so loud. Chipper stared into the darkness. Something was wrong.

Five minutes more and then leave.

Still nothing. The silence was beginning to unnerve him. He'd missed Roger. It was time to go. Then a noise came from directly below. He started to call Roger's name, but waited. Light rustling and someone was about to push open the hatch. He thought of the stranger that morning with Craig and Doog.

He took a chance. "Roger?"

Even in the dark Chipper could just barely see the door opening.

"Chipper? Are you there?"

"Yeah, yeah it's me. Thank goodness you got here. Where've you been?"

"You were late. I decided to check the hole."

"I couldn't come till my dad got home."

"It's okay now." Roger pulled himself onto the tree house floor. "I'm pretty sure the thief hasn't been out here tonight. I checked the hole and the same stuff from yesterday was there. I can't tell for sure though. Where's your flashlight?"

"Forgot it."

"That's not good."

"What's in there, Roger? In the hole."

Roger was quiet a second. "It was hard to see with the flashlight I have, but mostly stuff like watches and jewelry. Plus, what looks like a coin collection. I didn't take it out and look at it, but I think that's what it is."

"A coin collection? When I was in Cabrerra's garage talking to Kristy the other day, I saw a coin collection there. In a big book-like thing?"

"Yes, yes. A big thick book of coins."

Was it just a coincidence? The coins were in a box along with some Indian arrowheads.

Roger spoke again, "We should get to the fallen tree. Did you bring anything to eat?"

"Not really. Sorry. Tell me how this is going to work again? What do we do next?"

"I've changed the plan a little. Tonight we watch and see what happens. Practice for the real thing. We'll go to the fallen tree, wait for the guy to come, and see how long he hangs out. I timed the run to the phone booth. From that spot it's about ten minutes. Remember, you don't have to do anything unless something goes wrong. Then in that case, I just need a back-up witness. I will try to get the police to meet me at the field and then I'll bring them to the hole. Hopefully the thief's still there. That's why this has to happen fast. As soon as I see him coming, I'll start running for the phone. Tonight, I just want one more time watching. See what you think."

Taking a deep breath, Chipper nodded. "Sounds okay. When do we go?"

"Right now, but next time we go earlier. We can always just wait there. Let's get going."

Roger crawled over and reopened the hatch door. Flashlight in hand, he started down. Chipper followed.

"I wish I had that flashlight."

"Next time, make sure."

The last step was coming loose and it twisted on the tree trunk, Chipper almost fell. Roger was already jogging away. "Wait up," Chipper whispered loudly. He ran to catch up.

Roger clicked off the flashlight.

Where did he go? Ahead, he could hear Roger running. In those dark aisles, would they stumble into the thief? Maybe they were being watched right now.

Roger stopped to get his bearings. He clicked on and off the flashlight to show himself to Chipper. Ahead, the outline of eucalyptus showed against the sky. Roger turned on the flashlight for an instant, and played it around, searching for the right tree.

"Over here," he yelled in a voice that seemed too loud.

A few steps further and they came upon the huge eucalyptus that had fallen during some windstorm. It was leaning against another big tree. Roger handed Chipper the flashlight and worked his way up the trunk. He turned back around and Chipper handed him the light.

Roger made it look easy. He climbed right up. What happens if the tree's too hard to climb? With a thick branch Chipper found a toehold and boosted himself off the ground. Branches from a neighboring tree were everywhere and he was only able to make it a few feet up.

Stopping, he called. "Roger! I can't see."

"Just a sec, let me get a comfortable spot and then I'll give you some light."

The sound of rustling branches and leaves gave evidence of Roger changing positions.

The flashlight clicked on illuminating Chipper. Blinded, he had to close his eyes. Roger shifted the light from Chipper's face to a lower angle. He could see what to do. Grasping branches, he pulled himself up near Roger's perch. "Is there room for me?"

"Yeah, come on. There's room for two. Find a comfortable spot."

Chipper reached for a big branch that seemed like it would support him. He put his weight on it and tried to relax his tense muscles.

"Okay, now what?"

"We wait."

CHAPTER 18

There must be a more comfortable position. He
shifted his weight again. It was lighter out. The Big Dipper
stretched out directly overhead. He searched for the moon.
If it was out, he couldn't find it. Below were the vague out-
lines of orange trees. If someone were nearby, he might hear
them coming, but they'd be hard to see. Roger's plan meant
leaving Chipper here while he ran to the phone. That was
the next time, but he felt nervous thinking about it. Next
time, bring a flashlight.

The waiting continued. Roger seldom spoke, and the
discomfort continued. Was his left leg falling asleep? Afraid
to move. He might lose his balance and fall to the ground.
What was below? The fallen tree's branches were mixed in
with the tree it was leaning on. Hard to tell which tree was
which. Have to move. Straighten out the leg. It was getting
numb and hurt.

Roger whispered, "Don't move! Hear that?"

Chipper was half-standing. He froze and listened, turning his head in several directions. "No," he whispered back.

"Keep listening."

He didn't move. Strained to hear.

A muffled rattle came from behind them.

"There," whispered Roger.

Chipper looked back over his shoulder, but it was too dark.

The rattle moved closer. He held his breath. The intruder wouldn't pass directly under them, but in a row of trees not far away. So quiet. Nothing but the soft bang, bang. The thief's haul from that night. If either of them made a noise, they'd be heard for sure. His muscles tensed from bracing. His left leg ached. The sound of footsteps and the soft shifting and now footsteps moved from behind to the front. Was that heavy breathing he could hear?

Roger touched Chipper on the arm. "Wait," he said in a low voice.

Chipper was in no hurry to get out of the tree, but his foothold was slipping.

Seconds later, Roger tapped Chipper's shoulder and pointed to the ground. "Let's go."

Getting down the tree was harder than getting up. Roger hadn't turned on the flashlight and seeing was difficult despite the increasing moonlight. Chipper was in the lead. He kept low, holding onto the trunk as much as possible. Branches swept across his forehead and his left shoe came untied. Jumping to the ground might be easier, but what was below? Chipper landed among a pile of dead leaves.

"You okay?" Roger called.

"Yeah."

"Look out, I'm jumping too."

Roger leaped and, as he fell, gave a light groan, then he rose and brushed himself off.

"You alright?"

"Crap. Bit my tongue. Let's get as close as we can."

Bent over and taking slow, careful steps, they moved tree by tree toward the hole. Ahead, all quiet. Careful not to step on something, Chipper noticed a tiny spark of light through the tree branches. He smelled cigarette smoke. Roger slowed. A light shone in their direction. Had they been detected? He prepared to run, but Roger remained in place looking at his watch. There was more banging. Was he hearing the boards being removed or maybe put back?

What was Roger thinking?

Suddenly Roger dropped to his belly on the ground. Chipper did likewise. They pulled themselves under the lower leaves of an orange tree, avoiding open space. The smell of cigarette drifted past, but no light came from where the robber worked.

Chipper rested his chin on the back of his hands. What was he lying on? Must be an orange. The juice was smearing his pants. He pushed it out of the way. Next to him, Roger pulled nearer to the tree. What are we doing? Still couldn't see anything at all.

A new sound.

Back in the grove somewhere and coming closer. Possibly a voice. Behind them. Like before, but different. Did Roger hear it? Chipper couldn't see him very well, but did he just turn his head? There it was again. Roger twisted to look this time. Chatter, louder, but who? Sounded like two people.

Whoever it was, they were coming right toward them. He pulled himself further under the tree. Would they see his legs sticking out? He pulled them to his chest.

There were two people for sure. Talking back and forth. A flashlight bounced beams off the trees. They were getting brighter. He focused on staying still, took a breath and held it. Striding legs showed as they walked past. The voices. He recognized them. It was Rodney Kruger and Benny Gross.

Chapter 19

"C'mon Chipper, let's move up a little and see what they're doing.

"You sure?"

"Yeah, they won't see us. Be careful though."

"Okay, you go first."

Roger carefully raised himself from underneath the tree and eased slowly toward the voices. Chipper followed closely. Roger stopped and crouched. Chipper moved in beside him, peered ahead and turned his ear toward the voices.

Rodney and Benny arrived at the meeting place, a figure in the dark rose to greet them.

"It's about time you got here. I'm tired. I want to sleep you know."

"We tried making a run out here twice this week, but ran into problems and so here we are." Kruger walked up to the open hole. "Plus, we haven't completed all the deals yet. We need more time."

"Yeah. Hey Manx, we're selling a lot of your stuff, but we gotta be careful, you know," added Gross.

"Careful, don't tell me about careful." The one called Manx's voice grew loud and angry. "How much more time do you need? You two told me you could pull this thing off! Now, I've got doubts. I need to get out of this area soon. To do that, I need cash. How much do you have for me?"

"About five hundred after our take," Kruger replied.

"Okay, okay," Manx replied in a lower tone. "Not bad. I have some new stuff for you and then I need to get out of here. Make some deals, I don't care how you do it, but sell as much as you can. In a few days, I need to move on."

"We know a guy that might buy everything that's left. Hopefully anyway. We are meeting him in a couple days. We just wanted to make sure we knew what you have out here." Kruger moved closer to the bag and the big hole in the ground.

Manx waved his hand at the bag. "Go ahead, check it all out. There are some good takings you haven't seen."

Rodney and Benny shined their lights inside the bag then spoke quietly to themselves. They checked in the hole to see if there was anything they'd forgotten. Then Benny took the canvas sack and placed it inside.

"One last deal." Manx rose and reached for the boards to cover things. "If you guys can get most of it sold quick, you can keep the rest."

"Cool!" Benny looked at Rodney.

"Yeah bitchin," added Rodney. "We can do it. Here's your money. We'll meet back here in two nights."

"Good." Manx reached into his pocket and came out with cigarettes. "You guys want a smoke?"

"Sure," came the reply. Manx handed them a cigarette and then lit a match for them.

Roger and Chipper hadn't moved from their hiding place under the orange tree. Chipper heard most of the conversation, and it seemed Rodney and Benny were in partnership with the man they called Manx.

Roger nudged Chipper on his shoulder. "Time to go."

Moving slowly and trying not to make a sound, they crawled and then stood cautiously back up on their feet. The conversation of the three thieves was still audible. Trip now or step on too many dry leaves and it would give them away. The grove at night. The smallest of sounds carried through the calm air. Partially holding their breath and taking one short step at a time, Roger and Chipper relocated to a safe distance.

Reeled by the appearance of Rodney and Benny, Chipper blurted out, "Can you believe it!"

Still wary of discovery, Roger put his finger to his mouth. "Shhh, I'm thinking. They knew his name. Manx. I never thought about anybody else. This might change things. I mean, I hate those guys, but I go to school with them. When they walked past us, it shocked me. Rodney and Benny are selling the stuff. You heard them talk, right?"

"Yeah. I'm sure that's what they said. I heard it. Something about getting rid of all the stolen stuff. They gave him money and promised to sell the rest, I think. I am not sure, I didn't hear everything. Roger, maybe we should call the police now. What happens if they get away with this? This Manx guy leaves town. What then?"

"Yeah. I don't know." Roger rubbed his neck. "I'm not sure what to do. I don't want to be known as the guy who sent Rod and Benny to jail, even if they deserve it."

Chipper nodded. "Right, but what?"

Roger continued. "Let's get out of here. Tonight turned out a lot different than I planned. I wanted to time things, but when Rodney and Benny showed up I just stopped. I wonder how often they meet. How did he find them?"

"This is bad, Roger. Kruger already hates me."

They found their way out of the grove. In the distance they could see the glow of the streetlights that led the way back to Chipper's house. Once they left the shadows of the grove, Chipper split off in one direction, Roger in the other.

"I'll get back to you soon Chipper. Thanks for helping. See ya later."

"Okay, yeah. Later. I'm tired. I'll be around. Bye."

At the front of his house, was a moment of panic wondering whether his dad checked on his room. He hurried his pace toward the bedroom window. Sliding it open, nothing seemed amiss. Heaving himself through the opening, he fell onto the floor with a thud. With care, he put the screen on, partly closed the window and changed into pajamas. Under a sheet and a light blanket, he hoped sleep would bring a halt to the thoughts of Benny, Rodney, and someone named Manx smoking cigarettes together deep in the darkness of the orchards.

CHAPTER 20

The Fourth of July dawned on an unusually overcast day. Chipper's family and most neighbors planned attending the yearly fireworks party at the end of their street. Sometimes a picnic was included, but this year nothing formal had been organized. In the past, everyone contributed to the fireworks, which took hours to fire off.

Chipper anticipated finding Kristy to tell her about the events of the prior evening. Later, he would round up Doog and Craig, and get what money he could and go to the fireworks stand. He had enough money to buy a few boxes of "snakes", Piccolo Petes, and sparklers.

First, he was hungry for breakfast. He sought out a box of cereal and sat studying the sports section of the Orange County Register. Mind wandering, he remembered the voices in the dark of Benny and Rodney, reminding him that Roger would need a new plan. How would that work? Maybe just give up and call the police. What would happen to Kruger and Gross? Would they know he was helping Roger? Hopefully Roger would protect him. But for how long?

Better to tell Kristy. She'd know what to do. He rinsed his bowl, glanced at his work list for the day, and ran out the front door. He found Kristy in front of her house watering some rosebushes that bordered the driveway.

"Chipper!" she exclaimed. "I need to talk to you. I've been gone, you know."

"I know, I know. I came looking for you and figured you'd be back for the Fourth. And I've wanted to talk to you, too."

Kristy began again in a hushed tone, "What's happened with you and Roger? Anything?"

Chipper paused. Should he tell her about last night? In the end, he knew he would, including the part about Benny and Rodney.

For the next ten minutes, Kristy kept watering and Chipper told the story. Kristy's eyes opened wide when he came to the part about Rodney and Benny. She was as surprised as Chipper had been.

When he finished, Kristy responded, "Man! You guys are brave. Are you sure you shouldn't tell somebody? Somebody like your dad?"

"Yeah, I know, I've thought of that. The problem is the whole thing is Roger's idea. I'm just helping. You're probably right, but he would have to do it. Not me. Last night he wasn't sure what to do. Maybe he'll change his mind about the whole thing."

Kristy let out a long breath, moved the hose to a nearby tree, and said, "Someone tried breaking into our house last week. They didn't get in, but they cut a few window screens and dented the back door. The police were here and talked to my parents for a while."

"Wow, I know. I saw them, and guess what? Before

that, Doog and I saw Rodney at your front door. I'm not sure what he was doing, but maybe he was checking your house. I'd bet that guy Manx is involved. This is getting scary." Taking a deep breath, he added, "We can't keep this a secret much longer."

"The Cabrerra house was broken into a few days ago, too, you know." Kristy pointed at their home.

"Yeah? Guess what?" Chipper looked across the street at the Cabrerra's. "I think Roger saw some of their stuff in the hole."

"Nobody really knows when it happened. They were out of town for a week and came back to find a bunch of stuff missing from the garage, and it looked like someone had tried to pry open a house door from the garage. My mom and dad went over to talk to them and they think he broke through a garage window. They saw footprints in the dirt below the windowsill. He didn't go in the main part of the house. At least they don't think so."

"This is too weird. I need to let Roger know about all this. I don't know if I can help him. Maybe we can change his mind."

"I know. You're right, Chipper. I'll help talk to him if you want."

"That's a good idea. I need to forget about all of it for a while."

Across the street, the Cabrerra house made him feel uneasy. Tonight would be fun. Forget about Rod and Benny. Think about Roger later.

He changed the subject. "I'm going to check out the firework stand today. Want to come? I think Doog and Craig are going."

"Hmm. Let me think. I've bought some stuff already. If you do go, come get me. I have some friends to call."

"Okay, sounds good. I'm gonna find Doog and Craig and I'll see you later."

"Bye, Chip."

Chipper rang the doorbell and waited. The door opened and Doog's Mom appeared. "Hello Chipper, are you looking for Doog?"

"Is he home?"

"No. He and Craig ran off somewhere to get fireworks for tonight. I'll tell him you came by."

"Yeah. Thanks."

Figures. Wonder where they went. Always seemed like they went without him. Walked right past my house on the way. At least Kristy was back. He would go find her again. Craig and Doog would be at the fireworks party tonight. So would Kristy. He'd rather be with her. Seemed more loyal. Like she actually cared about what he was doing, thought, or cared about. Chipper wished they were in the same grade. After summer, then what?

He walked down the street and searched again for Kristy. Her friends weren't home when she called, so she happily joined Chipper on the walk to the grocery parking lot and the Black Panther Fireworks stand. Chipper bought boxes of wire sparklers and scanned the other more expensive fireworks.

With money left over, they wandered to the Tastee Freeze where Chipper liked the large root beer floats. Kristy bought a soft vanilla cone and they took their treats to a booth with red benches near the front window. While they ate, two adult women who were waiting for their orders spoke in loud voices. "There will be traffic up and down these streets. You can be sure of that. All those people coming and going. It'll be like that every day. And ambulances, too."

Chipper looked at Kristy and they smiled. This lady was really fired up about something. Chipper shrugged showing he'd no idea what she was talking about.

The woman continued speaking. "Something should be done before it's too late."

"Yes, you're right," responded the other woman. "Maybe we should talk to our city councilman, or if that doesn't work even, speak with Mr. Ramos. He lives here, too. Maybe he hasn't thought about the problems this hospital will mean for the neighbors. There must be other places for a hospital to be built."

Kristy stopped eating her cone and looked at Chipper without saying anything.

He started to speak, but one of the women began again. "Can you imagine all that construction going on? All those trees would have to come out and it'd take months to finish. Maybe years. The streets would be a mess."

Then it was silence as the two received their order and walked out the door. Chipper looked over his shoulder and watched them leave. "Are they talking about the grove across the street from us? Where the tree house is? I wonder if the Grove Man owns more than one orchard. I don't think he'd let anyone dig up his trees. He takes such good care of them. He's always in there working."

"Yeah, but maybe he's going to get a bunch of money."

Chipper stared into his root beer float and envisioned a huge building where the perfect rows of trees now grew.

There was a shopping center built near his cousin's house. It was a grove once, too. It could happen. He'd seen the evidence already.

Early in the evening, Chipper spotted Craig and Doog at the end of the street. Tables were unloaded and set up for the block party. Doog's father stood in the middle of the road preparing an old metal table for the fireworks. Most families already brought their fireworks and dropped them off into a big box set to the side. Adults sat on lawn chairs eating dinners brought from home, and watched the comings and goings.

Craig opened a box of snakes. He lit three and everyone nearby watched as the black ash grew out of the small charcoal-like cylinders. Kids were intrigued to see how long the ash would grow, before it broke off. One of the smaller kids grabbed the ash and lifted it up to see if it would float. Doog lit some snakes on the curb making a black stain on the cement. His father came over and told him to find another place to set them off.

On the Fourth of July, the rules for matches and fire pounded into him all year vanished. Every one of his friends had a pack of matches tonight.

After the talk with Kristy he'd thought about the grove and Roger a few times. Best not tell Doog or Craig anything about what he and Roger were doing. He trusted Kristy, of course, but not Doog or Craig.

Craig was allowed out of his yard for the first time since getting into trouble with the Grove Man. Between lighting snakes, he asked Chipper, "You been out to the tree house?"

He thought for a moment. "Yeah, a couple of days ago.

I was there. Everything looked okay. We've been lucky nobody else has found it."

"My parents put all the groves off limits for the rest of the summer. Maybe I'll wait a while and then see if anything changes. I don't wanna get grounded again. I'm sick of working around the house."

Doog spoke up, "Hey, did you guys hear about Kristy's and Cabrerra's? Someone got into Cabrerra's and tried breaking into Kristy's too. The police have been down the block a lot lately. You noticed?"

"When did this happen?" asked Craig. "Who told you this?"

"When they were gone on vacation. I heard my parents talking. My mom is all scared and everything and wants us to get a guard dog." Doog laughed.

Chipper chimed in, "Well, it's creepy." He wanted to tell them. He knew a lot. Too much. No, couldn't tell them. He had to stop thinking about it. Worry about it tomorrow.

The sky grew darker and the adults prepared to set off some of the fireworks. Different types large, small, cones and fountains, now filled a big cardboard box set in front of the open area. Lawn chairs circled nearby. Behind them, most of the younger kids waved sparklers. Parents encouraged them to be careful.

The older kids celebrated farther down the block with their sparklers. The sparkler burned toward the bottom of the wire and off it went, thrown into the night sky. It produced a flying projectile of light that often burned out in mid-flight. Parents warned them not to throw the sparklers, but it came across half-hearted and everyone threw them anyway. Occasionally one fell in a bush or next to a car, but they'd quickly be retrieved and thrown again if it were still lit. Chipper remembered once or twice a sparkler landing on a roof, and even on the hood of a car, but they quickly burned out.

From the end of the block, an adult male voice shouted, "We're starting!"

His friends walked in Chipper's direction. Doog yelled, "Let's go."

All four held lit sparklers and in a group advanced toward the end of the street. After a few paces, a bright burning sparkler hit the asphalt in front of Kristy. She stopped and glared behind her. "Hey! Whoever threw that, watch it!"

The boys ducked when another surprised Craig and the boys yelled a collective, "Hey!"

A second later, a burning sparkler flew near the adults. The four friends searched in the dark for the perpetrators.

"Is it those little kids over there?" asked Chipper, looking at a group of younger kids on the sidewalk behind them.

"I don't think so," said Craig. "Their parents are right there."

A bright flame of sparks and fire shot up from the box where the fireworks were stored.

"Let's find a seat on the curb," Doog suggested. They approached the circle of chairs. "Looks like they started."

The adults near the big box leaped up and moved away, yelling something that sounded like a warning. Chipper wandered where the first fireworks were about to be lit. Something wasn't right. Simultaneous flashes and sounds of shrill Piccolo Petes going off one after another poured out of the cardboard box.

Everyone in front stood, backing away, and grownups were herding children to safety. "Get back!" they yelled.

With a massive whoosh, the whole box went up in a firestorm. Chipper stepped away, shocked to see the entire collection of fireworks firing off at once. The end of the street lit up. Hot sparks shot everywhere around him and everyone else. Neighbors backed quickly from the growing inferno. One man nearly knocked Chipper over as he rushed by with his young son in his arms.

Kristy came up next to Chipper. "Holy Crap! What happened?"

"They are all going off at once, it's the whole box! It caught fire."

Someone yelled, "Get a garden hose over here!"

Groups of people took off running. Kristy and Chipper stood frozen as everyone's fireworks burned up by the growing fire. He looked over his shoulder to see where Craig and Doog might be, but in the panicked crowd, he lost sight of them.

"They can't find a hose, Chip, I'm going to go look."

She ran to where adults searched in vain for a hose in the dark. Finally, the owner of the nearest house ran head on for the flames, a hose in-hand, water coming from the nozzle. He rushed towards the box. The frightened crowd opened a path for him, but he stopped abruptly, the hose reaching no further than the end of his property. He shot the sprayer at the fire anyway. Some of the water reached its target, but it wasn't enough, and the blaze continued.

Chipper searched the crowd for Kristy. The glaring firelight was blinding. The noise from dozens of fireworks going off all at once, made it impossible to yell for her. He stepped out of the way into the shadows and scanned the front yard where he'd last seen her searching for the hose.

He suddenly caught sight of something else. Observing the spectacle from between nearby houses, four figures stood by themselves. At first, they appeared to be a family from one of the nearby homes, but then laughter. He kept watching, but here was Kristy emerging from where she'd disappeared a few moments ago.

"There's no way." She approached. "They're going to burn up for sure. I can't believe it. How'd this happen?"

"Kristy." He pointed to the place where the laughter had come from. "Who's that over there by the side of the Barron's house?"

She turned. One of the four held a cigarette lighter, lit a sparkler and threw it in a high arc towards the crowd. It landed near a man carrying a bucket of water towards the fire.

Chipper spoke first, "See that? They're throwing 'em at people. Did you see the face before he threw it?"

"I think so. It was Kruger, wasn't it?"

She squinted. "Yeah, it's him."

CHAPTER 21

There are no homes to burglarize for Manx this holiday. The Fourth of July fell on a Wednesday. Most are home. His two helpers searched for a vacant home, but someone usually answered the door. The holiday was easy pickin's. Finding a residence gone for a day or two was simple in the summer, but not this year. Time to move on. Find a new place to work.

Lately he had become suspicious. It was the stash hole. What wasn't right. Did it have to do with Rod and Benny? Not a thing was missing though.

He went to check his stash again tonight, just in case. When Manx reached the dead tree, he took his time unearthing his hiding place. He searched carefully with the flashlight for anything unusual; he scanned the ground near the tree. His loot was as he left it. Still, the doubt, the suspicion that somebody else knew…

Manx sat smoking a cigarette, staring at the dirt he'd piled back on the boards that covered the hole. He had an idea. With the flashlight, he'd find something that would work. In the soft dirt, he saw a dirt clod about the size of his fist. He placed it about the middle of the hole. There was no way to uncover the boards without moving the clod.

He thought, One more day, maybe two, and then he would leave. Even if Rodney and Benny couldn't sell everything. He'd take it with him and sell them to someone else. He was tired of their excuses. He didn't trust them. Soon, he would be gone.

He finished the last of his cigarette and then stood and got ready to leave. He flashed the light one more time on the clod. It had better be there when he returned.

Chapter 22

The morning after the Fourth of July fire, Chipper caught sight of Doog and Craig approaching his house. He threw on some shoes and ran out the front door to meet them.

"Hey Chipper," yelled Craig. "You want to go to the tree house? We haven't been in a while."

"Yeah, sure, but I thought you couldn't go in the grove." Chipper looked at Craig.

"I know, but if we just go there and nowhere else, I think it will be okay. I want to see the tree house," said Craig.

"You guys have the key?" asked Chipper.

"I got it," said Doog.

They turned toward the grove at the end of the street.

Walking amongst the trees, Doog began talking about the night before. "So my dad says he's pretty sure someone threw a sparkler and it landed in the box of fireworks. It must have set one off, and then the whole thing just exploded. I went and looked at where it was burning, and there's a big black spot in the street."

Craig said, "My parents asked me if I'd been throwing

sparklers and I told 'em I was with you guys way down at other end of the street. But I could tell they were still upset. My mom kept saying how lucky we were nobody was hurt. I guess that's true."

He took it all in. Should he tell them what he and Kristy saw?

"Kristy and I saw some older guys throwing sparklers. One of them was Kruger, I think. Not sure. Anyway, it could have been them."

"Yeah, that figures." said Doog.

"Was Benny there, too?" asked Craig.

"Not sure. They were in the dark, between some houses. He's usually with Kruger."

"Don't want to see them around. Ever," said Doog. "I'd like to see 'em get arrested or something."

Chipper nodded. "Yeah. Me too."

It was hot and dry, no breeze. Everything still and only the partial shade of the trees kept them from feeling the full heat of mid-day. As they approached the big avocado tree supporting their tree house, Doog reached into his pocket for the key. He climbed up the first few rungs of steps, skipping over the broken one and inserted the key.

Once he had the lock off, he pushed open the door and popped his head through the hole in the floor. "Hey, that stuff is still here."

Chipper kept quiet as he followed Doog up the tree and through the hatch. In one corner was the sleeping bag. There was also a pillow and an old t-shirt. Doog found a flashlight underneath it.

What was a reasonable explanation? Nothing came to him.

Craig entered. "Is this your stuff, Chipper?

"No, not mine," said Chipper. What had he already told them? Anything about Roger? Or nothing?

"Then whose?" Doog checked to see if anything was under the sleeping bag.

Tell a little of the truth. "It must be Roger Bell's. I told him it would be okay to stay here overnight if he wanted to."

"Why would he want to stay here? He's got the bitchinest tree house of anyone in his backyard." Doog eyed Chipper.

He shrugged. "I'm not really sure why. He just asked if he could and I thought it would be all right with you guys. Should I've told him no?"

Craig and Doog glanced at each other. Craig finally said, "Naw, it's all right, I guess. He wouldn't wreck anything. I don't really know him. I guess you know him the best, don't you?"

Hesitation. "I hardly know him, either. Just that one time he helped Kristy and me with Kruger and Benny. I see him around once in a while."

Doog broke in, "Isn't he, like, going into tenth grade?

"Yeah, I think so," said Chipper. "I know he's in high school." He needed to change the subject. "I have an idea. I was wondering if we should add on to this." He pointed out one of the windows and up at the roof. "Like, put another story on somehow."

"Yeah, that would be cool," said Doog. "But how would we get to the upper part—another hatch?"

"I guess." Chipper said, scrutinizing the ceiling. "Let's get on top and check it out."

Craig boosted himself onto the ledge and climbed out a window, stepping on a big limb. He crawled on the plywood roof with Doog and Chipper behind him. They stood on the limbs envisioning how a second story might be added.

"I don't know," said Doog, "I think we could do it, but it could add too much weight to the first floor. Plus," he gestured to a limb just over his head, "That limb would have to be removed. It's in the way, and I'm not sure we could cut it down without it falling on the roof."

Chipper and Craig nodded.

"Yeah, you're right," Chipper said.

They looked for a shady spot and sat. Craig laid all the way back, his head resting on his clasped hands. He closed his eyes.

Stretching his legs, Doog smiled slightly at Chipper and asked, "Chipper, did you know your mom got pulled over by the police the other day and they had her take a drunk driving test? She was arguing with them, and I guess it was really funny. I heard from Craig's brothers. They were there."

Craig opened his eyes and sat up on his elbows looking at Chipper. Chipper's body suddenly grew warm. It tingled. He was about to answer when Doog continued, "This was right in the middle of the day. She got pulled over by Walker's Market on 17th."

He hadn't seen this coming. Was this the only reason they had come to get him? His forehead began to sweat. His throat tightened. What to say?

With concentration, he composed himself, and staring directly at Doog, replied casually, "My mom takes pills for pain. She has bad headaches and has to take them all the time. She must have taken too many. I've never seen either of my parents drink."

This last statement was true. He'd never actually seen his

mother drinking alcohol. She drank secretly, hiding wine bottles everywhere in the house.

Doog and Craig looked down and then back at Chipper. He thought about adding more to his lie, but by Doog and Craig's reaction, maybe they were satisfied with his answer. With his voice shaking, he took a deep breath and, without Craig or Doog noticing, slowly let it out.

After leaving the tree house and heading for home, they stopped and picked oranges to throw. Craig had challenged Doog to a throwing contest aimed at an old, abandoned wheelbarrow. From twenty-five yards away, they threw seeing who could hit it first. Both Doog and Craig came close with their first two throws, but Chipper hit it square on his first and second throws. Then, Doog moved up a few feet and hit one of the handles. Craig kept missing and then charged the target out of frustration and threw until his oranges smashed into the rusting metal. Craig laughed at his inaccuracy and complimented Chipper on hitting it first.

"Dang, Chipper, both Doog and I throw harder, but you have better aim."

Chipper didn't respond, but threw two more oranges at some eucalyptus trees some distance away.

After a half hour, they reached the end of the grove and watched for cars as they set to cross the street. To the left, Roger and Kristy were walking together about a hundred yards away. He'd reached the sidewalk when Roger waved toward him and yelled, "Come here!"

Doog saw them too, glanced at Chipper, and said, "That's Roger, right?"

"Yeah, that's him," he said softly.

"What do you think he wants?" Craig chimed in.

"Don't know." Chipper walked in Roger and Kristy's direction.

"Hi, Chip," said Kristy.

"Hey guys, I need to talk to Chipper alone," Roger yelled as Chipper walked closer to him.

Both Doog and Craig paused. Then, without saying anything, turned, and started back in the other direction.

Before they got too far. Doog stopped and looked back over his shoulder. "Hey Chipper. See ya. Right?"

"Yeah, Doog. I'll see you around."

"Hey, guys." Chipper came to a halt beside Roger and Kristy.

Roger seemed nervous. He looked around to see if anyone was watching before he spoke. "I pretty much told Kristy everything that's going on. Seems like she knows most of it already though," he said to Chipper, who nodded.

"Anyway, I've decided that tonight's the night we try to get this Manx guy busted. Are you ready to do this, Chipper?"

He hesitated, but found himself saying, "I think so."

Kristy spoke up, "Hey guys, I've been thinking. I should come, too. Like to help Chipper, just in case something goes wrong. Chipper, you wanna wait in that dark orchard all by yourself. Really? What if the police don't come on time? I could wait with you. Doesn't that sound better?"

Chipper glanced at Roger and let out a quiet, "Ah, yeah."

Roger contemplated Kristy. "Hmm, I think that's okay. You sure you can get out of the house on time? You need to be at the tree house with Chipper at 11:30. No later. Right?"

"Yeah, I think I can."

"You have to be sure, Kristy," said Roger.

"Yeah, I can do it. I'll meet in front of Chip's at eleven. We can get to the tree house in fifteen, maybe twenty minutes, right?"

"Okay, that'll work," said Chipper. "But, what about Rod and Benny? Did Kristy tell ya 'bout last night?"

"Yeah, I heard. Let me take care of that. I'll do it right away. I should've before, but I wasn't sure what to do. Now I know. I'll tell you about it later. So, we all meet at the tree house by 11:30 tonight. I'll check the hole before that. I hope there's still stuff in it. If not, the plan won't work. Then, we all go to the fallen tree, wait till Manx comes, and then I'll run for the phone booth at the field. I can make it in ten minutes. I already practiced once. I hope the police get to me in say, five to ten minutes, and then I'll direct them to the hole. He usually hangs around for at least thirty minutes. The police can drive their car down that dirt road by the grove. Should be quick getting there." Roger paused. "Here's the important part for you. If the police catch Manx and arrest him, you can either come out and show yourselves, or quietly sneak away and nobody will ever know. Not even your parents. But if for some reason he leaves, or they can't catch him, I'll need you to back my story. This part can't get messed up." Roger made eye contact with Chipper and then Kristy.

Chipper didn't hesitate, "We'll be there, Roger. I promise. We won't leave." But if they do catch the guy, I'm sneaking back home. My parents would kill me if they knew.

"Mine too," added Kristy, worry showing on her face.

"Okay then, I need to go to the bowling alley. I'll see you guys at the tree house." Roger sped into the trees.

Chipper and Kristy turned to walk back home.

Standing in front of his house making the last plans with Kristy, his mother came out the front door and got into the red Chevy.

"Chipper. Would you open the garage so I can pull in?"

"Sure, Mom."

"See you tonight, Chip," Kristy said. "Hope we can do this."

"We'll be okay." He waved goodbye. He opened the garage and his mother drove the car inside.

The Chevy was never in the garage. Why now? His mother turned off the engine and Chipper pulled the big door down with a bang. "Keeping the car in the garage now?" he asked.

"Maybe for a long time," she answered.

"Something broken?"

"No. I'm not driving anymore. Maybe when you get older it can be yours."

"Wow! Really?"

"We'll see."

She walked to where Chipper stood and pulled him close. She looked down at him. "You know I love you. More than anything."

"Yeah. I know."

"Good. Never forget."

"I won't, Mom. I won't forget."

Roger greeted the front desk attendant upon entering the Hillview Bowling Alley. He strode directly to the back of the darkened building, where three pinball machines were positioned. Playing happily at two adjacent games were

Rodney Kruger and Benny Gross.

Roger walked up to the clanging machines. He leaned across the glass top and spoke in a quiet, firm voice. They listened without a word, still pushing the flippers.

Shortly, both boys stopped playing and slumped over, studying Roger. He finished talking. Still neither spoke. Holding up his index finger and pointing at them both, Roger stared down Rodney until he looked away, and then he focused his gaze on Benny. Both mumbled something in return and nodded their heads.

Roger turned and retraced his steps toward the entrance. Rodney and Benny shuffled away from their unfinished games and sat in two plastic chairs with their arms folded, frowning.

Out the front entryway, Roger waved to the man behind the front desk who said, "Have a nice day."

"I will," he replied.

Chapter 23

From bed, Chipper stared at the fluorescent-lit clock. It was 10:50 p.m. Under the covers, he wore Bermuda shorts and a long sleeve t-shirt. Was Kristy watching her clock too? Maybe she'd changed her mind. Was Roger already in the grove, checking the hole? Was this a bad idea?

It was too late to change his mind, especially since both Kristy and Roger were counting on him. What about the plan? So many things could go wrong. He could always run. Run as fast as he could to his home and crawl back in the window. Across the hall, his parents' bedroom door was closed and he rose to get ready. He had the flashlight in-hand. He puffed his pillows making a lump. Did it look like he was asleep under the blankets? Maybe.

Slipping out his bedroom window late at night had become routine for Chipper. Work the screen off and place it inside. Boost himself on the sill and shift his legs to the other side. Jump down and then listen for noise inside. Did anyone hear him? Any neighbors outside? He moved warily onto the sidewalk. Was Kristy coming? Peering into the darkness, no Kristy. He waited. What time was it when he got out? She wouldn't be late. Must've changed her mind. He walked back to the window, attempting to see the little clock inside. It was after eleven. Where was she? Back on the sidewalk, he gazed again toward Kristy's house. Then he saw her.

She was waving at him. He waved back.

"Sorry, Chip. I had a terrible time getting the screen off. It was stuck. Oh, my God, I had to go out the front door. I don't think anyone heard. I hope not. "Am I late?"

"Yeah, sorta. We gotta go fast. Need to hurry to meet Roger in time."

Kristy grabbed Chipper's arm. "I'm so nervous."

"Me too. But we have to get going."

Together they jogged down the sidewalk towards the grove and the talking stopped.

"After we get past the streetlights, it's going to be pretty dark," said Kristy with a frown, as she peered into the blackness.

As they entered the first row of trees, Chipper grasped the flashlight from his back pocket and pushed the on button.

"Crap, the batteries are low." He banged it in frustration.

"Roger will have one. Right?" whispered Kristy.

"Yeah, usually, but he'll take it with him to the phone. He's gonna kill me, but we can't go back now. Maybe there's an extra one in the tree house. I saw one today."

With apprehension, Kristy and Chipper kept up a quick step down the first long row of orange trees

The night's warm air included the slight sensation of a midnight chill coming. Running through the freshly tilled dirt slowed their speed. Was it darker than the previous nights? Where was the moon? The moonlight made navigating in the dark so much easier. Now landmarks were hard to recognize.

Kristy looked back over her shoulder. "Do you think Roger will be waiting?"

"He could be checking the hole. Isn't that what he said he'd do first?"

"Yes, that's right, I hope he's at the tree house when we get there, though. I can hardly see where I am going."

"Are you afraid?" Chipper asked.

"Yeah, of course. Aren't you? But, if I weren't here, you'd be doing this all by yourself. Have you thought about that?"

"Of course. You're right, I'm really happy you're here too. It'll make things so much easier, especially later. I just hope Roger knows what he's doing."

"Would you rather have Craig or Doog helping you?" Kristy turned down one of the many rows they passed by.

"Forget that," said Chipper quickly. "I trust you way more than either of them. You kept this a secret like you said you would. Plus, I don't think either of those guys would've even come. No, Kristy, you're the only one I'd want to be with tonight. Thanks a lot."

She laughed lightly. "Yeah, I must be crazy or something. I hope everything works, 'cause I just want to sneak back home later. My parents would kill me if they knew what I was doing. I don't even want to think about it."

"I know what you mean. Unless Roger needs someone to back up his story, let's get out of here quick."

Kristy nodded. In the distance, a dog barked, and an automobile engine roared. The tree house closer, home farther away.

Plodding through the dusky orchard, without speaking, Chipper sensed they were close. "Turn left when you can," he said under his breath.

Kristy worked her way between two trees, then looking back, said, "You take the lead. I'm sorta lost. Are we there yet?" They stopped and searched ahead. Not yet. Chipper looked in vain for a landmark, something familiar. He started walking again in the direction Kristy had been heading. "We're close, I think. I wish I'd checked this stupid flashlight.

"Chipper? I have a question."

"Yeah?"

"How do we know, we won't run into the guy, Manx, or whatever, here in the dark?"

"Right. I know. I thought about that last time, too. If you hear anything, let me know."

Ahead he saw what looked like the clearing separating the two groves. The tree house was just around the corner and down a few rows. As he turned to tell Kristy the good news, a beam of light caught the lane just ahead. They froze in place. With all the trees in the way, it was impossible to see where the light was coming from.

Kristy put her hands on Chipper's shoulders, and then, leaning slowly forward, put her mouth to his ear, and whispered, "Is it Roger?"

Chipper turned his head and even though she was so close he could feel her breath on his cheek, he could hardly see Kristy's facial features in the dark. He muttered, "I don't know."

Kristy's fingers tightened their grip near Chipper's neck. "What should we do?"

He shrugged and gradually squatted.

Kristy followed him to the ground and they took a knee.

Ahead, the light bounced as the person walked. Was the tree house only yards away? It had to be Roger.

He would take a chance. Staying low, Chipper moved towards the figure he could now hear approaching. Kristy followed close behind. The flashlight beam was just ahead. He was able to get a partial glimpse of the person who was moving along at a brisk pace. Kristy stood tall and called to him, "Roger, over here."

Chipper panicked, not certain it was him. The view was still mostly blocked by a tree directly in front of him.

Relieved, he heard Roger return Kristy's shout. "Where have you been? We have to get going."

"Okay, we're coming," Chipper said.

Without further conversation, the trio exited the clearing and began a brisk pace towards the fallen eucalyptus and the thief's cache in the ground.

Roger turned once and urged them to catch up, explaining that he was about to turn off his flashlight.

Kristy and Chipper struggled to keep up with Roger's quickness.

Kristy whispered, "Slow down, you're going to lose us!"

Roger waited as the pair caught up to him. "I looked in the hole, I don't think he's been there yet. I hope he shows tonight."

"Yeah, right," Chipper said back.

"Oh my God, what are we doing?" said Kristy.

"You okay, Kristy?" asked Roger.

"I guess."

"How 'bout you, Chipper? Everything all right?"

"I think so."

"Then stay close to me and be real quiet."

When they were at the base of the fallen tree, Roger directed them to climb. "I'll be at the bottom, so I can get out of here fast."

Kristy crawled part way up the tree, but before Chipper could move, Roger grabbed him by the arm. "Shhh, don't move."

They stood motionless, listening. It wasn't far off. He couldn't make out the words, but someone was speaking. It came from the direction of the dead tree near the hole in the ground.

CHAPTER 24

Manx approached his hidden cache, his light searching for the large dirt clod he'd left, marking his hole. Lots of little clods but not the one he left. He crouched and peered closer. Could it be? The big clod was moved off to the side. Someone was getting into his stuff. They knew.

"Damn! Damn! Damn!" he yelled. Then, in a quieter voice, he added, "I knew it! I knew something was wrong!"

Frantically, he scraped the dirt from the boards, pushed them aside, and shined his flashlight into the hole, expecting it to be empty.

He was talking loudly to himself now. "I can't believe it's all here. Why aren't they taking something? I need to get my things and leave. Somebody knows. Is it Benny and Rod? I don't get it."

Manx's senses were on alert. He flashed his light around the grove, wondering if he was being watched. He listened keenly for any suspicious sounds.

In the distance, Chipper could see a bright beam searching the trees many yards away. Still nobody spoke. What was Roger thinking? What happens now?

Roger whispered, "Chipper, get up with Kristy."

Kristy had sat on some crushed branches. Chipper lifted himself next to her clinging to a thin branch where her feet rested.

Roger whispered, "I'm going, don't leave."

The sound of him running away communicated that Roger had decided to sprint for the phone and make the police call. After a few more quiet seconds, Kristy leaned towards Chipper. "Crap, I'm so afraid."

"Me too."

Manx loaded his bag with the remaining stolen items from inside his hole. He moved quickly, listening for any unusual sounds coming from the trees. Had someone been spying on him the whole time?

The bag was full. He pulled out a cigarette and lit it trying to relax before he left the grove. Who is it? Had Rod and Benny betrayed him? The loot was all there every time he checked. Benny and Rod sold his things and he kept track of what he gave them. Was there something he hadn't thought of?

He sat on the dusty ground staring at the uncovered pit.

"I'll finish this cigarette and never come back here," he said to himself.

"My leg is cramping," whispered Chipper. "I need to change positions."

Kristy nodded and tried to make more room for Chipper.

"Darn Chip, I can't hardly move either."

"I know, but I'm not on a very strong branch," he whispered back. Chipper's movement produced a rustle of dead leaves as he attempted to find a more comfortable perch. Then a loud "snap" sounded as Chipper's weight broke one of the branches. He cringed at the sound.

"Darn it!" said Chipper, "I can't see where to put my legs and I feel like I'm slipping."

Kristy groped at him. "Chip, grab onto my arm."

"I'm trying."

Branches snapped again, and Chipper hit the ground with a thump.

"Oh. No," she whispered. "Are you okay? Chipper—Chipper? You okay?"

"Yeah, yeah, I think so." He tried to stand up.

Above, Kristy scooted down the narrow tree trunk to the ground. She reached for him.

"How bad was that? Did he hear us?" he said under his breath.

She found his arm, grabbed onto it and spoke lightly into his ear, "I don't like this. Should we run?"

Manx heard sounds nearby: tree branches cracking, and then voices. He turned in the direction of the fallen eucalyptus. He clicked off the flashlight as he gradually rose to his feet, walked around the open hole in the ground, and took a few tentative steps in the direction the noises had come from.

"Somebody's out there," he said under his breath.

Kristy and Chipper stood in the blackness. Kristy felt for Chipper's hand. She tightened her grip and he squeezed back. Frozen in place, Chipper focused his attention on the shuffle of movement coming from ahead. Was someone approaching or maybe something else? He concentrated harder. Listening.

Kristy whispered in his ear. "Should we get back in the tree?"

He opened his mouth to respond, but the soft crunch of approaching footsteps in front and to the left jolted him. He tightened his grip on Kristy's hand, and whispered, "We need to go."

"What about Roger?"

"I know. But, we can't…just don't make any noise."

She picked up her left foot, avoiding dry leaves or sticks that might give them away.

Chipper's attention was fixed on the direction of the footsteps. Was a figure standing just a few trees away? Was it Roger? If he could only see better.

He turned to back away; Kristy shifted next to him. Down that row. Yes, he's there. Does he see us?

The flashlight beam didn't land on Kristy or Chipper, but in the dark orchard. It lit up everything around them. He faced the direction of the light, but was blinded. There was no choice. "Run!" he yelled.

Chapter 25

Chipper ran straight down the aisle of trees, no light, with Kristy just ahead. The only sound was hurried steps over uneven ground. He couldn't lose her.

She turned right and he wondered where they should go. Already he was disoriented. He didn't look back; he had seen them. Were they being chased?

Kristy was further ahead and he was having trouble keeping up. He shouted, "Hold up"!

Did she look back? Then, another turn between the trees. Chipper followed, brushing past limbs, sharp thorns cutting his bare arms. Kristy made another turn and he struggled to follow. Tempted to yell to her again, he'd have to slow down and catch his breath. A beam of light illuminated a branch above his head, appearing ever so briefly.

They rushed deeper and deeper into the grove. How long could they run before needing to rest? Gotta keep up with Kristy. What about Roger? There was nothing to do but keep going, get away from Manx and the hole in the ground. They had to find somewhere safe and get back home.

Kristy slowed. Chipper bounded up beside her. He bent

over trying to catch his breath, reached up and wiped his sweaty forehead. Their hard breathing disturbed the still quiet.

Between breaths, he said, "We need to keep going."

"Yeah, I know. Did we lose him?"

"Not sure. I don't see anything. No sign of any light."

"Chip, where are we?"

"Not sure. We go until we run into a street or something."

"What about Roger?"

"He didn't get back in time. Nothing we could do. Let's go and don't lose me."

"Sorry, I won't."

Encircled by thousands of fruit trees, they started jogging. Watching for light beams. The moon was rising, and grayish shadows were appearing. It was easier to see the outline of eucalyptus, and the long straight rows of orange trees. Water tanks and stacks of orange crates loomed in night. Chipper strained to hear distant cars, but it was late and any streets might be far away.

Kristy slowed to a walk. "Is it time to find our way back? I don't think he's following us."

'Yeah, we lost 'em. I think so anyway. The thing is, I don't really know where we are. I'm not sure how to get out."

"Okay. We can't go back the way we came. So what do we do?"

"Let's stop for a second and keep listening for cars. We've got to find a road."

Dead quiet was broken suddenly by a dog barking. They changed direction toward the sound. "A dog, maybe a house too. It's something. Let's go." Thought Chipper aloud.

The bright nearly full moon helped light their way past

row after row of short round trees. The bark of the dog grew louder. There should be streetlights ahead. A few minutes later, the dog was quite close, and Chipper wondered whether the animal was lost too. No lights, nothing at all but trees. Not one car engine sounding in the distance, but something was familiar. He'd been in this area of the grove before, with Doog and Craig. It was when they were looking for Dirty Charlie, and a grove worker caught Craig.

He called to Kristy, "Wait a second, I know where we are, sorta. There is a house ahead. That's where the dog is. Craig and Doog and I were here once. We got into trouble."

"Oh yeah, I remember you telling me. How do we find our way back home from here?"

"That day we just ran, like tonight. Not sure how I got back. It was light out then. We came out on Fourth Street.

Now, I'm all turned around. Maybe let's get closer to the house; that might help. Doog and I were behind a metal shed somewhere."

Kristy let Chipper lead the way. The dog stopped barking. Coming upon a small grove of young avocado trees, there was a light ahead. He stopped and listened. Just then a man's voice in the trees ahead called, "Hey, who's there?"

Chipper froze, straining to see who was speaking. Kristy kept walking. "We're lost." Her voice quivered. "Can you help us?"

CHAPTER 26

Chipper got ready to dash away, but having heard Kristy's response, he took a few hesitant steps forward.

The man spoke again in a friendly, easy-going manner. "What are you kids doing out here late at night? Your parents know where you are? Lost or something?"

The voice sounded like a much older person, but in the dark Chipper couldn't be sure. He moved closer to Kristy. "Someone is after us. We've got to get out of the orchard and back home. Where are we?"

Now, the man stood in front of them. He was wearing a bright red bathrobe and held a walking cane in one hand. He limped as he neared them. "You say you're running from somebody? Step over here near the front porch light so I can see you better. I live here with my dog, Jasper. He was barking so much he woke me up. I came outside to see what's going on. I expected a raccoon, not you two. What're your names?"

After introducing themselves Chipper and Kristy explained as best they could about Manx, Roger, and his plan. The man looked back and forth at them, and occasionally nodded. He asked a few questions and then when they were finished, let out a slow, "Whew," and added, "Darn complicated."

"Yeah, I know," said Chipper.

Finally, the old man spoke again. "Really, only one choice and that's to take you two to the police station and explain the whole thing. You probably don't like that idea, but I can't very well just take you home and drop you off. Wouldn't be right."

Chipper and Kristy pondered this problem, and after a while, Kristy spoke up. "What do you think Chip? We have to tell somebody. We don't know what happened to Roger. He could be in trouble. If he got the police to follow him into the grove, they probably didn't find Manx. I can't think of another idea and I'm so tired."

He was exhausted, too. The consequences of going to the police were awful. It meant calling his parents. He didn't want to think about that, so he just nodded at the man. "I guess."

The dark blue 1950 Ford pickup hardly had enough room for three passengers, but they squeezed on the bench seat. The old man turned around in the driveway and drove down the dirt drive.

On the way to town, Chipper recognized a few landmarks and some streets. They were in a part of town on the opposite side of the big grove. The truck took a right turn toward downtown. Chipper started to ponder what his parents would say when he called. He looked over at Kristy; her eyes were closed. She had to be thinking the same thing. Was there a way out of this mess? There must be, he just couldn't think of one. Too tired.

Minutes later, they turned into the police station and parked near the entrance. A big glass doorway led to a brightly lit waiting room.

Kristy saw him first. "Look, there's Roger. He's talking to somebody. Are those his parents?"

The old man peered ahead. "So, that's your friend?"

"Yeah, that's Roger. We better go in there quick. Something went wrong."

Chipper sighed and started toward the door, dizzy with thoughts of his parents coming to get him at the police station. Behind him, a weary Kristy walked slowly, staring at the ground.

Abruptly, the old man spoke up. "Hold on a minute, let me think here a sec."

Chipper looked back at the crumpled figure of the man leaning against the front of the truck for support. He motioned to Kristy and Chipper. "Come over here and let's talk."

Kristy looked puzzled but she turned to walk back to where the man stood. "We need to help our friend Roger. What else can we do?"

"Yeah, yeah. Right but I know a couple of those officers and I think I might be able to keep you two out of it for now. I can't promise anything, but let's take you home and I'll run back here and see what I can do. What do you think?"

Kristy eyed Chipper with a look that said, *Please say yes!*

He was numb and exhausted. Was there hope that his parents wouldn't get that phone call tonight? He could just go home to bed.

"Okay, you'll come back and help Roger?"

"Yes, yes, I'll do everything I can. I'll think of something."

"Okay, I guess. What do you think, Kristy?"

"I'm so worn out. I don't want to call my parents. Do you?"

"No. Me either. I just hope Roger is okay and he doesn't blame us later."

With that, Chipper and Kristy hopped back in the front seat and gave directions to their street.

Late at night, no traffic at all. Cruising past the orange grove where the long night had started, row after row of trees disappeared behind them. Approaching the turn that led to their homes, the truck passed a station wagon parked off the street next to the curb. Inside that car, a man took a long slow draw from a cigarette.

The light caught Chipper's attention and he stared back at the car. "Did you see that? The guy in the car smoking. Was it Manx?"

Kristy peered behind, "You kidding? Really?"

"Not sure, but sitting in a car in the middle of the night smoking a cigarette. And, right across the street from the grove."

The old man spoke up, "What do you want me to do? Should we go back?"

"Turn right at this next corner, and then we can go to the end of the street and turn right again and get behind him. Maybe I can sneak up and read the license plate number."

"What! I don't know Chip. You sure?"

"It's worth trying. I'll be careful. I want the license number and then we go. Is there a pen here somewhere? I can write on my hand."

The man turned as Chipper directed. "Look up on the dashboard."

Kristy leaned forward and grabbed a pen lodged between the dashboard and the front window. The truck turned right again and Chipper pointed to a big tree overhanging the street. "Park under that tree and let me out."

"Chipper, be careful, I'm worried." Kristy looked deep into his eyes. "Don't take any chances."

"I won't, It'll be okay."

Kristy opened the door. He scrambled past her and jumped out of the cab. There were five houses to walk past and then he'd come to the main street where the station wagon was parked. At the last house, he slowed until he saw the rear end of the car. There was a short wooden fence nearby where he could move up to without being seen, but after that, there was nowhere to hide.

How close did he need to get? Hunched over and moving quickly, he rushed to the cover of the fence. He waited a few moments before lifting his head to peek over. No sign of the man in the car, nothing, complete stillness. Can't make any noise at all. He moved to change the angle so he could see the plate better. Too dark. He needed to get closer. It would be easy to climb the little fence, but then what? Crawl up to the back of the car. He felt the pen in his hand. Should have tested it first. His mind was muddled. Would he remember the plate number and letters if the pen didn't work?

Climbing the wood fence, his pant leg caught on a splinter. Pulling it free caused a scraping noise and he ducked on the other side. On all fours, he was across the sidewalk and nearing the back end of the car when he stopped to look at the plate again. Was that RJB or BJP? The numbers were 459, or was the five a zero? He had to get closer.

The car started. The driver revved the accelerator. Chipper ducked and lay flat on the ground. So close. Does he see me back here? The headlights turned on; the license plate light flashed on too. The numbers were rusty and faded. He put out his hand and wrote. RJP 408. The pen barely worked. The clunky station wagon pulled away. He tried again. No ink. He turned to run and repeated to himself RJP 408. The car gained speed.

The pickup came down the street. Do they see me? He kept running. The truck engine roared to life and, without headlight lights, rolled into the middle of the street.

Was it RKP 408? No, that's wrong. J not K.

Kristy opened the door. "Did you get it?"

"RJP 408. Yes, I got it."

"Now, I'm taking you home. Right?" said the man.

"Can you remember the license number?" asked Chipper.

"Yes, I hope so. Did you write it down?"

"Pen didn't work. RJP 408."

"Got it. Where do we go from here?"

"We live a few blocks away. Thanks for helping us," replied Kristy.

The truck stopped near the end of their street where Chipper and Kristy hopped out.

"Okay, home with you. I'm gonna head downtown and see what I can do. If you can find my place again, come out in a few days, and I'll let you know what happened."

"Thanks, we will. Please help Roger, okay? And, we don't know your name," said Chipper.

My name is Charles and I'll do what I can. You get home."

The door closed, the man turned the truck around and

retraced his route to the police station.

Chipper and Kristy hurried in the direction of their homes. Chipper's house was closest. It seemed like forever since he'd met Kristy out in the front yard earlier that night. Looking east…was the sky getting lighter? A new day was starting.

"Sorry I got you mixed up in this," he said in a slow, heavy voice.

Kristy stopped, "Chip, I begged to go, remember? Maybe everything will work out. I can't think straight right now, I only want to sleep." She reached out and hugged Chipper, holding on tight.

He shook his head. "If you hadn't been there. I don't know."

At the end of the street, the newspaper guy was working his way toward them.

"We better get inside." Kristy let him go and started along the sidewalk. She stopped and turned back towards Chipper, who was walking up his driveway. "Chipper?"

'What?"

"You know who that old man was, right?"

"What?" said Chipper.

"The old man. I think he was Dirty Charlie. You know?"

Chipper stood, preparing to jump onto the windowsill. "Hmm." He nodded. Yeah, I guess you're right."

Chapter 27

It was late August. Soon, Chipper would begin his second year in junior high school. Seventh grade. Kristy was going into eighth. He'd only seen her sporadically since the long night in the grove. He hoped to see her today, the first day his parents had given back his freedom. Kristy's parents kept her close by and busy. He knew she was home. He'd seen her in the front yard. Would her parents even let her talk to him? He'd find out.

He walked out the front door without telling his mother where he was going. That was new. For weeks, he had to explain everything he was doing and why. But not today. When he reached the sidewalk, Kristy was crossing to the Cabrerra's house. She picked up the hose and turned on the faucet. Must be watering while they're away.

She turned to see him coming. "Oh God, Chipper!"

"Hey, Kristy."

"Can you leave your yard?"

"Yep, today I'm free again."

"I've needed to talk to you so bad. I wanted to find out what happened to you and Roger and everything, but my parents…you know."

"Yeah, me too."

"So, tell me. How did things turn out?"

"I was in so much trouble. For a while nobody spoke about it all, but then I heard my parents talking and guess the police caught Manx a few weeks ago. They tracked the license number."

"You were right then. It was him that night."

"Yeah. Charles, Dirty Charlie or whatever, must have told somebody, but I'm not really sure what happened to Roger. Did you see the newspaper that week?"

"I know my parents were looking at it and talking but I never saw it. Did you?"

"No not really, but I heard my parents say something about our names not being in the news. I think Roger was though."

"He's probably mad at us."

"Kristy, what could we have done differently?"

"Nothing, Chip. I've thought about it a lot."

"You still grounded?"

"Not sure. What do you want to do?"

"I'd really like to go out to the tree house before school starts. What do you think?"

"I probably won't tell my parents that."

"How about we walk to the ball park and then cut over to the tree house from there?"

"Okay, that'll work. I'm almost done watering and I'll meet you on the corner."

"Cool. I'll get permission and see you there."

Rather than return home, he kept walking to the corner. Might be easier to just wait there. Mom might have questions about what he was doing. Ahead, some workmen were putting up a sign in front of the orchard. Too far away to see what it said, he watched them work while he waited.

The men completed the work and drove off in a big truck loaded with construction gear. He was about to walk across the street to read the sign when Doog and Craig popped out of the grove. Seeing Chipper, they ran over.

"Wow, Chipper, it's you. Can't believe it," said Doog.

"Yeah, finally can leave the yard."

Craig smiled. "Is everything we keep hearing true? You, Kristy, and Roger helped catch a burglar, some kind of criminal…or what?"

"Well, sorta. Really Roger did. Kristy and I ended up getting into a lot of trouble. That wasn't the plan, but the police discovered I was somehow involved and came to our house the next day. My parents freaked out at first. I had to explain the whole thing. Got in so much trouble."

"We heard some guy was chasing you with a knife, or was it a gun?"

"He was chasing us, but I don't think he had a knife or anything." Chipper shrugged. "Maybe he did."

Kristy approached the three, and Chipper said, "Kristy and I are going to the park. We haven't been able to do much. Been pretty boring."

"Hi, Doog. Hi, Craig. I can go Chip, you ready?"

"Cool. See you guys later."

Craig punched Chipper's arm in a friendly way. "Come by and let's hang out, Chipper. Oh, and Doog and I were at the tree house the other day. There's an envelope just lying there. It has your name on it. If you go there, you'll see it. Weird huh?"

"Hmm. Sure it's for me?"

"It's your name," said Doog. "Looks like something's inside, too."

"I'll look for it. See ya guys."

Kristy and Chipper crossed the street and walked toward the big sign that now stood before the line of eucalyptus. The sign read in large letters:

COMING SOON
New Horizons Hospital and Clinic

Below that was a list of different contractors and other companies involved in the project. The sign said the hospital would be completed in October of 1965.

Chipper frowned. "Does this mean all the trees? Everything? Even where the tree house is?"

"I don't know. I guess there'll be a huge hospital right here. They'd just tear up the whole grove?"

A bright yellow bulldozer sat partway down a nearby row of trees. Nobody around. He walked to where it was parked. Kristy followed.

Chipper climbed to the driver's seat. Preparing to sit on the black metal seat, he heard a shout, "Hey! You don't belong up there! Off you go!" A man in a construction helmet motioned at them.

"Ooops, sorry," Chipper yelled. "I wasn't going to mess with anything."

The man approached and seemed friendlier. "I know, but I can't have anyone playing around here. I'm gonna start hereabouts, so be careful and stay back. There will be others coming and you'll need to stay out of this whole area. In one week this entire section of grove will be dug up."

"Everything?" said Kristy. "How far are you going? "

"All the way to the next line of eucalyptus. Gonna be a brand new hospital here." He climbed in the seat of the bulldozer and waved them away. "I'm gonna start this engine and see how this is going to work. Not sure if we'll need some different machinery to get these trees dug up."

Hearing the engine roar, Kristy and Chipper took a few steps back. The bulldozer moved toward the closest orange tree. The enormous metal plow dropped to the ground and it scraped the dirt in front of the tree. With little effort, the powerful tractor shoved the tree, roots and all out of the ground.

Kristy and Chipper watched until Kristy said, "Do you think you could find the old man's house again? I think we should go there instead. We should thank him."

"I might. I know the direction. I wonder if they'll tear down the avocado tree where the tree house is. Let's go by there first."

"Yeah, okay."

Minutes later, they approached the area near the tree house. At first everything seemed normal, but closer to the enormous tree, they discovered another bulldozer set off to the side in a small clearing. Five orange trees were already torn out by their roots and lay together to one side.

"I can't believe it." Chipper gazed at the vacant space left by the trees. "What's that tied around the tree?" he added, seeing a bright orange ribbon looped around the base of the big avocado. "What's that mean?"

"I think it means, don't cut this down or maybe, cut it down. It's one or the other."

Chipper stood under the floor of the tree house. The

lock was off. Soon he was inside. Roger's dirty sleeping bag was still on the floor. He recognized the same old candy wrappers lying around. Kristy hauled herself inside. The envelope Craig told him about lay on the floor. On the front was written, "Chipper". He opened the envelope; a paper fell out.

"What's it say?"

He held up the paper. "Chipper—Sorry I got you and Kristy into trouble. The police asked so many questions I had to tell the truth. I'm glad they believed me. Thanks for your help, and tell Kristy thanks, too. Roger."

"At least he's not mad at us, Chip."

"Guess not. Glad of that."

"Roger's plan worked you know. The part about catching that Manx guy."

"Wish our parents hadn't found out, though."

Chipper peered out a window. Kristy leaned beside him. From their perch high up, they stared down on the tractor. Young avocados hung on a limb nearby. Beside the downed orange trees, loose oranges were spread over the ground. In the distance was a long line of eucalyptus trees with the same orange ribbons tied to them. Faintly, the sound of a bulldozer growled across the expanse of orange trees.

Kristy took a deep breath. "Chip, the old man's house? Which way?"

"That way, I think." He pointed.

"Let's go."

Made in the USA
San Bernardino, CA
14 May 2018